Karen L. Syed

Moonlight for Maggie

Echelon Press

Publishing

Moonlight for Maggie
An Echelon Press Book

First Echelon Press Production / September 2012

Echelon Press, LLC
2721 Village Pine Terrace
Orlando, FL 32833
www.echelonpress.com

ISBN: 978-1-59080-732-3

Published by Echelon Press LLC

Other works by

Karen L. Syed

~ **Novels** ~

Lost and Found

Dark Shines My Love

~ **Short Stories** ~

Seducing Cupid

Devlin's Wicked Wish

An Angel's Wish

Thief of Hearts

Too Fast for Love

For Moghis.

Every day I find a new reason to be happy.
I thank God for all my blessings.
I thank God for you.

This book was written at a time in my life when I had
no idea if I would survive.

Special thanks to everyone who has stood by me
through every adventure, misadventure, and difficult
time I had to endure:

Alysen Waller
Carolyn Rogers
Tammy Wing
Mark Schabbes

My most heartfelt appreciation and respect to
Caroline Bourne.

Reading your books and living your stories made me
want to be a good as you. You inspire me and your
friendship means the world to me.

And if you are reading this, thank YOU for taking the
time to read my work. I hope that something in these
pages touches you in some way…that isn't creepy.

One

"If it were any smaller, I'd need a magnifying glass." Maggie Howell stared at the man standing in front of her. Noticing the flushed and exasperated expression on his face, she smiled. Gracing him with her best coquettish look, she brushed the wayward curls away from her face.

"You're overreacting, Maggie."

Maggie loved her job and she'd do what she had to in order to earn her money, and maybe a name for herself. But even this was asking a lot.

"Maggie, it's the best I can do for you."

"Joe, you can't really expect me to do this under these circumstances. It's a blatant waste of my experience. I've got a lot more to offer than this is worth." She walked across the room and stared out the window overlooking Shreveport.

"Here's the money and everything else you'll need."

Maggie turned back to him and accepted the envelope and small plastic pouch. Staring down at them, an odd sense of anxiety overwhelmed her. It still amazed her she could get paid for doing what she loved. She more than earned the money on every call.

Not once though, had she ever worried whether or not she was good at what she did. Of course I am, she reminded herself silently. Her job had taken her into the private chambers of some of the state's most influential men. None had been disappointed in her performance.

"Maggie, are you all right?"

Joe's voice startled her and the envelope slipped out of her hand, falling to the floor. When she stooped to pick it up, her watch chain caught on the black stockings she'd just bought. A thin run shimmied up her calf.

"Crap!"

"I really need you to do this, Maggie."

Straightening up, Maggie sighed. "I can't believe I'm actually going to do this."

She turned a scrutinizing gaze on him and continued, "What am I going to do when everyone finds out how low I've been forced to sink by the likes of you?"

Moving away from him, Maggie's foot caught the strap of her overnight bag, and she toppled against Joe. His arms wrapped intimately around her. She felt his chest rise and fall with each breath he gulped.

"I've dreamed of this for years, Maggie, but I always thought you'd like me when you fell into my waiting arms."

Maggie hastily pushed away from him. When she looked up at his face, she found his eyes sparkling with mischief. She swatted at him playfully.

Holding up the envelope, she winked. "It's just a good thing for you, I can be bought."

"I knew you only liked me for my money," Joe teased.

"I would have liked you even more if you'd found someone else to send to little, itty-bitty Port Ray. I've done bigger fluff stories than this."

"Maggie, I think you're underestimating the importance of this assignment. You were picked because you have a nose for digging out the meaty parts of a story," Joe consoled.

Frowning, Maggie held her hands in front of her. "I don't call small-town organized crime a big news flash. It's everywhere and nobody cares about it. I'm only agreeing to do this because you helped me get on with the paper. Plain and simple, I owe you."

"This has nothing to do with me. It came from the big cheese himself."

Her hands dropped to her sides and she smiled. "Mr. Atkins really asked specifically for me?" Maggie enjoyed the warmth of pride burning in her cheeks.

"Read it for yourself." Joe handed her a piece of paper and smiled.

Maggie read the words scribbled on pale blue office stationary. She glanced up at Joe, letting some of the disappointment of her latest assignment slip away. Even she couldn't deny the personal satisfaction of a request straight from the boss.

Maggie remembered her first meeting with Joe.

She'd pretty much bullied him into hiring her when she'd applied for the assistant reporter position at the Shreveport Daily. Guilt over her tactics led her to work grueling hours making it up to him.

She'd walked over a lot of people to get to this point in her career. Not something she was proud of, but she'd worked twice as hard to justify her actions. She'd sworn to never move so much as one little step backwards in her career. Small-time crime in Port Ray, Louisiana seemed like a giant step back. Maggie remained confident her talent should be carrying her to Washington, not to a hick town no one even bothered putting on a map.

"You have a local contact when you get there." Joe handed her a file folder.

Eyeing him suspiciously, Maggie opened the manila cover. "Paul Remington," she said thoughtfully. "Didn't he do a story on this for some local sheet?" She'd read his stuff before. Good reporting, but very emotionless. She could only imagine the kind of guy he'd turn out to be. "What does he have to do with my story?"

"He has an angle on Anthony Greely and his connection to the family. From what I can gather, there's some kind of feud between Remington's family and Greely's. Paul's determined to blow the lid on this one."

"So, you want to team me up with someone who has a grudge? That's nice, Joe."

Maggie leafed through the pages, making mental

notes. She'd do some investigating on her own and only use Remington if she had to. If she had to spend weeks in some hick town digging up dirt, she fully intended to get full credit for the story. No partnerships on this one.

"I'm gonna do this, Joe, but I'm gonna do it my way. On my own." She knew she was pushing him.

"Just make contact when you get there. I'm going to be checking up on you. Try to keep in mind, that I *am* still your boss." Rubbing his temples, he leaned against the edge of his cluttered desk. "Two weeks, Maggie."

"Really?" Glancing at her watch, she realized with surprise that she had less than an hour to make the flight Joe had booked for her. She'd make it though, since she didn't have any family she didn't need to tell anyone goodbye. "Guess I'd better get a move on. Time is money."

Paul Remington loosened his Tasmanian Devil tie as he paced the tiny office. His tennis shoes squeaked on the linoleum floor. Trying to ignore the annoying sound, he turned his attention back to his boss. "What makes you think I wanna work with a big-time, Shreveport reporter? I started this story, and I can damn well finish it on my own." Paul slammed his hand down on the desk. "I don't need some big-shot know-it-all breathing down my neck while looking over my shoulder."

"Paul, this reporter's got contacts you need. This

could be the ticket for you to get on with the Daily," Hal appealed.

"I can do it on my own," Paul demanded. "I've got as much, if not more, experience as most of those damn city reporters. Besides, what makes you think I even want to work for the Shreveport Daily?"

Rolling his eyes, Hal challenged him. "Yeah right. I know how appealing this town is, and I'm quite sure you want to grow old here. You can get fat and bald with the rest of us yahoos." Pushing out of his chair, Hal Parker moved to the file cabinet. He opened the top drawer and pulled out a stack of papers. He tossed them across the desk and they slid to rest in front of Paul.

"What are these?" Lifting the top few sheets, Paul skimmed the print. "Why do I need these? I'm not working with anyone else. I don't need to know what he wrote."

Sighing deeply, Hal sat back down. The old chair groaned in protest under the added weight. "You know something, Remington, that's your biggest problem."

The pseudo-antique desk chair Paul chose to sit in creaked as he spun around. His gaze landed on Hal's belly. He focused on a deep yellow mustard stain staring back at him. "What are you rambling about?"

"You're so close-minded. What could it hurt to give her stuff a look-see?"

"I beg your pardon?" Paul bolted up out of the chair, sending it flying into the wall behind him. *A woman?*

"Did I forget to mention, he's a she?" Hal grinned. "Silly me."

Paul's mouth dropped open and he shook his head back and forth. "You can't be serious. You want to send a damn woman in to investigate and crucify an organized crime family? How can you even begin to justify that?"

Paul jerked around, his elbow slammed against the corner of his metal file cabinet, and he cursed Alvin Greely and his slimy brother. When they'd cornered him at the courthouse earlier in the week, he'd been caught off guard. Nobody in their right mind roughs up a reporter at the courthouse. Then again, the Greelys had never been in their right minds. Even in their youth, all the brothers had been loose cannons. It didn't help now that they were all grown and on the move. He rubbed the tender spot on his elbow. Packston Greely had power flowing through his veins. He never passed up a chance to show the kingpins he had what it took to run with the pack.

Paul had been in Port Ray all of his life and had no intention of letting the mob take over. Even if the fools thought they had a right. They were small time hoods and Paul figured he had a responsibility to let the rest of the town know it. New Orleans had been a hot bed of mafia activity for as long as anyone could remember. He knew, realistically, he could do little to change things, but he'd sure as hell die trying.

"Work with me on this, Paul. I need the story and the exposure could do us both some good. Atkins is one of my oldest friends and he wouldn't send this woman if she wasn't the best. Just meet the lady and see what she has to offer."

Locking his gaze on Hal, Paul made his opinion clear. "I don't like this one bit, and I resent you manipulating me this way."

Paul could get past the partnership, but as far as he was concerned, women had no business messing with organized crime. No matter what. He had better things to do with his time than babysit a prissy little fluff writer who wanted to make a name for herself.

After stuffing his papers into the worn leather briefcase, Paul left the small one-story building, and headed for his brother's place. As he drove, he devised a plan. He'd meet with this reporter, give her some of the gorier aspects of his findings, and she'd run back to Shreveport with a tummy ache. He'd do what his boss asked, and then some. He didn't so much have a problem with women working, but certain things should be left to the men. Men shouldn't stay home with the babies, and women shouldn't mess with the mob. That's just the way things should be.

Maggie stepped into the small-town bar. Stopping, she gave her eyes a moment to adjust to the change in light. She'd been walking along the main drag, checking out the town. The bright lights and sparkling signs painted a portrait of a miniature New Orleans. When she'd spotted the old wood-carved sign, *Chaser's*, she'd decided to go in.

Maggie felt the thumping of the Cajun music throbbing through her body. Port Ray was a far cry from Shreveport. It was simple, almost quaint. The two-story wood building pulsated with passion around her, years of history etched in the walls. She smiled at the perky blonde waitress behind the bar and returned her wave. Couples sat at several tables scattered around the room. Most kept their heads together, and very few looked up as she made her way across to the bar.

When she approached, only one stool sat empty. Next to the vacant seat sat the most intensely good-looking man she'd ever seen. His sandy brown bangs swooped down across his forehead. Raising her hand, she fought back an unwelcome urge to brush the locks aside. She was saved from total humiliation when his hand absently brushed them back, exposing noticeably indifferent eyes.

Maggie stepped up and motioned toward the stool. "Is this seat taken?"

Barely glancing in her direction, he ignored her question.

A flicker of light caught the silver flecks around his pupils and she stared. Maggie assumed she'd imagined the spark of something in his eyes before he glanced away.

"It's empty, sweetie," the waitress said, smiling at her. "What can I get you?"

"Thank *you*," she stressed, glaring at the rude stranger.

Maggie slipped the strap of her bag over the back of the stool. It tipped precariously when she let it go. Struggling to stop the chair from falling, her elbow knocked up against her neighbor.

"Ouch! Would you mind picking on someone your own size?"

Momentarily taken aback, she stepped away from him. *Well*, Maggie snickered, *another point for friendly Port Ray*. It seemed a shame for such a handsome face had to be marred by a scowl. She watched as he emptied his glass.

"Bonnie, can I get a refill?" The man slid his empty glass across the bar, and scribbled something on the legal pad in front of him without even looking up.

Maggie wondered what had upset him and caused the wrinkle across his brow. He glanced her direction. She stopped breathing when his deep blue eyes locked with hers. Totally and completely mesmerized, she stared.

White-hot chips of ice flashed in the depths of his stare and her insides melted into liquid fire when he smiled at her. The warm smile contradicted the chill of his gaze.

"Sorry."

Maggie shivered as the baritone strains of his voice plucked the strings of her composure. Unable to think of anything even remotely intelligent, she lowered her head, hoping the dim lighting would hide her embarrassment.

Within the flash of a second, his attention moved

onto another man who'd appeared behind the bar. She listened quietly as the two men talked.

"Holt, I don't know what I'm supposed to do. I started this whole thing, and I really don't understand why Hal's making me pair up with someone else."

"Look, little brother. You're the one who wanted to stay here in Port Ray. You know how everyone thinks. Anyone who's still here will always be here. I get the feeling you're ready to move on with your life, and I think Hal's trying to help you out."

Maggie watched the man empty his glass for the second time since she'd arrived. He slammed the glass down on the bar. "She's a damn woman."

The sharpness of his voice startled her and seltzer water sloshed over the rim of her glass.

The man behind the bar laughed.

"So, that's what this is all about. Your fragile little ego has a pinhole in it. You think this big town reporter is going to come in and make you look bad."

Momentarily blinded by the light shining in her head, Maggie soaked in this new bit of information. Here she sat, next to the man she'd been bullied into working with, on her story.

"Hey, I'm no chauvinist. I like women as well as the next guy, but I think they should know their limits. Why would a woman want to go and put herself in danger over something like this?"

"For the same reason you big strong studs do," the waitress chimed in. "It's an exciting rush."

Maggie accepted the fresh drink the barmaid set in

front of her.

"Thanks for the input, Bonnie Bell. This is a big help coming from the most exciting waitress I know."

Maggie's opinion of her neighbor dropped considerably with each word he said. She'd struggled against his kind of testosterone-induced mentality for years, trying to work her way up to lead reporter. Male reporters had the mistaken impression all women were frail and helpless. She'd struggle valiantly to dispel the theory proclaiming all women intellectual idiots. No man would tell her she couldn't run with the big dogs. She'd done more than her fair share of fluff stories, and now it was her turn to shine.

"Don't bust her butt, Paul. She's right. Women are pretty much capable of doing anything we can."

Maggie looked at the man behind the bar and smiled at him. "Better," she mumbled. She relaxed when he winked at her.

"I'm sorry, did you say something?" Paul turned on her.

"I think her drink is too strong."

Maggie sighed with relief, thankful for the bartender's intervention on her behalf.

"Well, since she's right here, let's ask this pretty little lady next to me what she thinks," her new partner suggested.

Maggie shuddered at his condescending tone and fought down her urge to slap the smug look off his face. Why did men always have to draw the battle lines with the gender issue? Sure, she was a woman, but the way he said it made it sound more like a curse than a blessing.

"Ask me what?" she purred at him in her sweetest drawl.

"What do you think about women doing dangerous jobs, *chère*?"

Smiling sweetly, Maggie lowered her lashes. "Well," she said softly, "I can't imagine what I'd do if I didn't have some big strong man to do all those horrible things for me. I think it's a man's job to protect us."

"There you go, Holt. I rest my case."

The man behind the bar crossed his arms over his chest. "What do you do for a living, Miss…?" He looked at her questioningly, "If I'm not being too personal."

"I'll bet you're a secretary in some big fancy office. Right?" Paul smacked his hand on the bar and smiled.

Maggie considered her words very carefully, allowing herself time to cool down. "What would you say if I told you I worked as a construction supervisor on an offshore rig for a major oil company?"

"Big fat liar," Paul said teasingly. "You're far to pale and pretty to be in that line of work. You definitely fit the pencil-pushing part."

"Is that so bad?"

"Not for a woman."

"Okay, maybe I'm a lieutenant for one of Louisiana's most notorious crime syndicates."

"Yeah, right." Paul snorted.

"What do you do?" Maggie asked.

"I'm a field reporter for the local newspaper."

"How terribly exciting for you."

"Yeah, but you still haven't told us what you really do."

"My name is Maggie, and I'm the lead reporter at the Shreveport Daily. I'm in town to investigate the allegations of small-time mob activity."

Heat shimmied up Paul's neck until his ears ignited into flames of humiliation. Rotating his stool, he moved until he sat facing her. He considered what to say, feeling confident whatever he chose would not be accepted graciously.

"I'm Paul Remington."

She ignored his outstretched hand.

A chill swept up the length of his spine. "I guess you think I'm a real jerk."

"I guess you're a lot brighter than I gave you credit for, Mr. Einstein."

"Ouch! That's quite an attitude you've got there, *chère*."

"Yeah, well, it ain't diddley compared to yours."

Paul watched her silently as anger flashed gold in her hazel eyes. When she picked up her glass, he wondered if he would soon find himself wearing its contents. Instead, she drained the glass and slid it across the bar toward the smiling waitress.

"Well, Mr. Remington, you now know who I am, and I wish I could say it's been a pleasure meeting you, but I'm going to assume you are smart enough to know I'd be lying, so..." Her pink lips puckered seductively as she let the word roll slowly out of her mouth.

Opening his mouth to speak, he thought twice, and promptly shut it.

Spinning the stool around, she stood up. "Damn!" The strap on her bag snapped, sending it, and its contents, scattering all over the floor.

Paul sat perfectly still while she picked up the loose papers. She mumbled to herself as she worked and he thought she looked soft and whimsical. Not the type to sneak around dark alleys trying to find dirt on mobsters.

She pulled her bag against her chest and stood. "Thanks for the help. Don't ever let anyone tell you chivalry isn't dead." She turned to walk away, but stopped.

"What is it, *chère*?" Paul asked.

"I promised my boss I would make contact with you when I got to town. I have. Now, stay the hell out of my way."

Paul stared after her, speechless. Her jeans tightly hugged the lower portion of her body. The subtle sway of her hips, as she stormed across the room, set him on fire. He inhaled deeply, trying to recapture the smell of her perfume. He got a breath full of stale cigarette smoke for his effort. Her tawny brown hair blew back when she yanked the door open, and his spirits dipped dangerously low as she disappeared out into the humid night.

Staring blindly at the door, he considered going after her. Why? To apologize? Why should he apologize? He'd only expressed his feelings. He had a constitutional right to his own opinion, he'd be damned if he was going to be sorry for it.

"Well, Paul, I'd say you made quite an impression on her. I almost think she likes you."

Paul frowned at his brother, but held his tongue.

"She's quite a looker. Too bad you don't stand a snowball's chance in-"

Two

Paul stood up. "I don't give a hoot. She was sent here to make my life miserable, and I'd say she's going to excel in that capacity. She's already off to a great start." He drained his glass. Waving goodbye to his brother and the waitress, he stepped out of the bar into the night.

Pulling the collar of his shirt open, he headed toward the parking lot. After slipping into the pickup truck, he sat and waited for the air conditioner to cool off the cab. When he finally pulled out of the parking lot and headed home, his thoughts stayed on Maggie Howell.

He turned onto Wilder Avenue. Hazard lights winked at him through the light mist of the early September rain. He stopped the truck next to her and rolled down the passenger side window. "Need a hand there?"

She turned around and frowned when she saw him. "Good Lord, what else?"

Not the greatest form of ego boosting he'd ever seen. "Well?"

"Sure, you can cut off your left one." She dipped

her head back under the open hood and ignored him.

"Are you this hostile with everyone, or am I just blessed?"

"Blessed? I doubt it," she snapped.

He parked the truck in front of her car and stepped out into the mist. "What's the problem? Do you need a jump?"

Nothing.

She continued to tug on wires and wiggle things as if he wasn't even there.

"Maggie, let me help you out. I'll call a tow truck or something."

She spun on him and he had to catch her when her foot slipped on a spot of wet oil. As he held her in his arms, the moist chill he'd felt disappeared, replaced with a heat so intense it overwhelmed him.

"What's wrong, Mr. Macho, you can't climb right in and fix it yourself? I thought since you're a man, you could do anything."

She pulled free of him, and his foot slipped.

He took a deep breath to counteract the pain shooting through his arm as it buckled under the weight of his falling body. His head smacked against the street, and everything went dark.

When he woke up he heard the voice of an angel, well not exactly.

"Dear lord, I've killed him."

Paul lay perfectly still, listening for any signs of concern in her voice. Maggie hovered over him.

"Paul, are you all right? Come on, wake up."

His eyes opened and hers closed. She hovered over him so close her breath warmed his face. Watching her carefully, he tried to decide if she looked thankful or sorry he still lived. She held his face in her hands as she talked to him, giving each cheek a couple of quick pats. At least she hadn't wrapped her hands around his throat, to choke him. It has to be a good sign, he thought.

"You can stop slapping me. I'm fine."

"No, you're not. You hit your head when you fell. I thought you'd seriously hurt yourself."

"And slapping me stupid will make me better?" Paul watched her cheeks flame.

"Don't be stupid, I just wanted to wake you up. *Are* you hurt?

Paul tried to form a smile, but pain shot through his head with the effort. "Just my pride. I don't spend much time falling at women's feet. Especially women who are-" Paul stopped before he made more of a fool of himself. No way would he admit to her that she'd really stoked a fire in him.

"What? Women who are what? Strong? Independent? Self-sufficient?" Maggie got to her feet and glared down at him. "I should have let you lay there."

"Are you always in the habit of jumping to conclusions, or do you actually read minds?"

"I don't need to read your mind to know you are intimidated by strong women."

"You're not strong, you're mean."

"You don't know anything about me."

"Look, you're right. I don't know you and I shouldn't have said anything.

"You're right. You should have kept your Victorian viewpoints to yourself. I should have known when you hit your head, you wouldn't be hurt."

"I said I was sorry. What do you want from me?" He struggled to sit up, trying to rub his head at the same time. The pain in his arm kept him from following through on either.

"Look, do you want me to call an ambulance or something?"

Paul shivered when the humid warmth of the southern night vanished, and the chill of her attitude surrounded him. He stared at her mouth. Her lips looked soft and sweet and he seriously considered kissing her just to make her be quiet. Common sense told him, despite the Louisiana heat, he'd die of frostbite in the road if he tried.

The direction of his thoughts grated on his already injured pride as he struggled to stand. "I'm fine; I just slipped. If you help me, I'll get up and give you a lift home. You can pick your car up in the morning." He waited for her argument, but none came. She leaned down, offering her hand to help him up off the ground. He perused it for weapons before taking it.

After locking her car, he moved to open the truck door for her. Before he had a chance, she climbed in and slammed the door.

"Women," Paul mumbled.

"I'm at the Regent."

When he pulled under the Regent's canopy, she climbed out of the truck and walked inside. Four words. She'd spoken four words to him. Not even so much as a thank you. He watched until he saw her step into the elevator. Then he sat a little longer. Paul shifted the truck into drive and pulled out onto the road. He played back the events of the evening in his mind and reached his own conclusions on its outcome.

"She likes me."

Jerk! Maggie stormed into the hotel. Her mother would have cringed at her rudeness. Well, it didn't matter. Her mother was dead and she was completely on her own. She had nobody, no entanglements, and it suited her. Pausing, she wondered, *Don't I?* As she made her way across the short lobby, she glanced toward the full-length mirror next to the elevator door. Paul sat in the truck, staring after her. Her heart raced as she picked up her pace.

Knowing he sat watching her made the walk from the truck to the elevator painfully long. "Why does it take these things so long to move?"

"I think it's the distance it has to travel from top to bottom."

Startled that someone had heard her talking to herself, she glanced over to find a stocky man standing several feet away. "I'm sorry, I thought I was alone."

"Oh no. You'll never be alone."

Not sure what he meant by his comment, Maggie

chose to ignore him. The elevator door slid open and she stepped into the small compartment. When she turned around to push the number four button, she saw Paul, still staring at her. As the doors slid together, she caught a glimpse of his face before they closed her in.

Was he trying to intimidate her? *Well, forget it, Buddy.* Sagging against the wall, she closed her eyes and counted to ten. She found little comfort in knowing she'd remained in complete control until he slipped out of sight. She opened her eyes and looked down at her hands, shaking like leaves in a windstorm. Well, it didn't matter. She'd die before she'd let some Cajun hillbilly know he'd gotten to her.

She stared at the markings on the panel walls. Although the hotel claimed to be the best in town, it still left a lot to be desired in the elegance department. The door slid open and she walked toward her room where she noticed a box leaning against the door. Who could have sent her something? She stepped up to the package carefully and stared down at it. Duncan's Floral Depot. "Joe, you silly man." She bent down and picked up the box. *You* better *feel horrible about sending me here.*

Maggie wiggled the plastic card key in the lock until the handle finally turned. "Damn electronic keys. Doesn't anybody remember brass?"

She flipped the locks on her door before tossing her bag on the bed and laying the flower box next to it. She stepped around the bed and pushed open the French doors. A cool breeze rolled into the room, a remnant of the earlier shower. After taking a deep cleansing breath, she moved to the bed and picked up the box. Impatiently, she tore the red ribbon from around the package and flung the lid off. How long had it been since anybody had cared enough to send her . . . Her eyes bulged as she stared down at the box. Not long enough.

Her chest throbbed as she gasped for air. Painfully, the muscles in her throat clenched and the room swayed around her. *Please, God, don't let me faint!* Her mind screamed at her to put the lid back on the box, but her body remained paralyzed. Every time she moved her hands to reach for it, her stomach heaved. Her quivering knees barely held her upright. She wanted–no, needed–to sit.

It wasn't until several of the horrible bugs crawled out of the dead orchids onto her bed that she found the strength to scream. Her lungs burned with the effort of sustaining the sound as the room spun around her.

Bang. Bang. Bang.

"Hey, open the door."

Startled by the pounding, she hesitated before forcing herself to move away from the bed. Her hands shook as she struggled with the door locks. Finally, it opened.

"What's going on in here?" Even as she threw herself into Paul's arms she felt him peering around her into the room. "Maggie, what the devil is wrong?"

"It's horrible. They're everywhere. Make them go away." She waved her hands frantically and panted for air. She closed her eyes trying to make herself calm down. Horribly enough, bugs were one thing she had no tolerance, or stomach for.

"Calm down. Tell me what's wrong." Paul tightened his arms around her and she felt his hand smoothing her hair down around her head. Something in the way he held her assured her that he would protect her.

But only from the wretched bugs, she thought fiercely. That's the only protection I need.

Stepping away from him, she avoided looking at the bed. Scraping her fingernails against her bare arms, she struggled to make the itching stop. Had they gotten on her? She swatted at her clothes and shook her head, certain that hundreds of the insects clung to her hair. Tingling sensations on her scalp taunted her with her own weakness.

"Maggie, stop it. You're hurting yourself." Paul grabbed her hands, holding them so she couldn't scratch any more. She struggled against him. He held her until she found the courage to point toward the bed.

He left her standing by the door and walked across the room. "Maggie, what is this?" Paul held up several of the dead flowers and bugs fell from the plants. Tossing them down on the bed, he dug through the box. Finally, he pulled out a small square card and read it to himself.

"Paul, tell me what it says." Maggie took a step closer, but movement on the bed stopped her from going any closer. "Tell me!"

"Let's just say it's not from an admirer." He tucked the card into his trouser pocket and grabbed her bag off the bed. He shook it several times and once satisfied it was bug free, he held it out to Maggie. She stood still, refusing to touch it. A few shakes weren't enough to convince her no nasties crawled around on the inside.

"Oh, for cripes's sake, Maggie. They're more afraid of you than you are of them."

Maggie forced a smile. "Don't bet the farm on it."

He looked at her with one eyebrow raised and chuckled. "Well, it appears Miss Independence does have a weakness."

Maggie hated the patronizing edge to his words and her anger flared. "Get out!"

Paul hesitated for a minute, and stepped toward the door. He reached for the handle, and she panicked. He wouldn't dare leave her alone in a room full of bugs and dead flowers.

"Wait! Where are you going?" She grabbed his arm, her nails digging into the sleeve of his shirt. He gave a little tug and she loosened her hold. "You can't leave me here without getting rid of-" She pointed toward the bed and her skin crawled. "Them."

"I hadn't intended to leave you here at all, until you told me to."

"What *were* you planning on doing?" It suddenly occurred to her that she might question why he'd come after her in the first place. The sound of another voice in the hallway outside her room stopped her.

"Look, I think you might be better off someplace

else. Where's the rest of your stuff?"

Maggie pointed toward the closet on the other side of the bed. "You aren't going to make me get it, are you?" Her stomach churned with disgust at the thought of having to go anywhere near the bed.

"No, I'm not. Just take your briefcase and go down to the lobby. Tell the bellman to come up and help me."

Reluctantly, Maggie picked up her bag. She wouldn't have touched it if it didn't have all of her notes and research in it. "Will you be long?"

"No, only as long as it takes to gather all your stuff. Don't talk to anyone except the clerk at the desk. I'll explain when I come down." He disappeared into the bathroom and she looked over at the bed.

"Thank you," she said quietly.

He poked his head out of the bathroom and smiled at her. Her heart raced. She forced herself to look away, unwilling to give away the warm feeling his smile invoked. She peeked out the door before stepping into the hallway, and then hurried to the elevator. Maggie glanced over her shoulder several times when she thought she heard someone, but she didn't see anyone except a maid.

Her ego stung from the intensity of her reaction to the situation, and she hated having shown weakness, especially in front of him. She fidgeted nervously as the elevator lowered to the lobby. When the doors opened, she looked around, didn't see anyone between her and the desk, and hurried over.

"Can I help you, Miss Howell?"

"I–um–there are–there's bugs in my room."

The clerk looked at her as if she'd grown a third head. "I don't think that is at all possible. We're very careful about those sorts of things."

"I'm telling you, there are bugs. Mr.–my friend is up there right now and he'd like you to send someone up to help him."

"Help him? Oh my, goodness." The desk clerk made a call and a bellman appeared, and then disappeared into the elevator. Less than fifteen minutes passed before Paul came up behind her. Pulling the desk clerk off to the side, Paul whispered something to him, and slipped him a folded bill.

A few minutes later, as they walked toward the truck, Maggie felt some of her control returning. Her heart rate slowed to an almost normal pace and the queasiness in her stomach settled to a dull roar. "Why did you give him money?"

Paul glanced over at her. "I wanted to make sure no one goes into your room. He agreed to change the setting on the door lock, so only he would have access to it."

"And you had to pay for that? I already paid for the room for a week."

"Everything costs extra. It's just the way things work."

"Are you going to tell me what the card said?"

"Not yet."

"I'm a big girl, I can take it. Obviously the florist

made a mistake and those flowers were meant for someone else."

"I don't think so, *chère*." His curt answers were really beginning to annoy her.

"Look, Remington, I've only been in town one day. I hardly think I could be the intended. I haven't had a date in over a year, so it can't be a disgruntled boyfriend." *Oh hell.* She hadn't meant to give him any information about her personal life, and now he knew she couldn't get a man. "And don't call me *chère*."

"The flowers were definitely meant for you. I wanna know why." Paul turned the truck into a long driveway.

Maggie sighed in exasperation. "Look, I'm sorry if I'm being rude. It's been a very long day. I'm tired and a wee bit cranky."

"Really?" he drawled sarcastically.

The slight Cajun drawl caught her off guard. When she looked over at him, their gazes locked. Something in his expression warned her to look away, but she couldn't. On the outside he appeared calm, cool, and collected. The dangerous passion she sensed smoldering beneath the surface threatened to be a different problem altogether.

"Why are you looking at me like that?" Paul thought for a split second she might smile, but the sound of the garage door making contact with the cement startled her and she visibly cringed.

"You just reminded me of someone for a second."

"I hope you like them better than you like me."

"I'm sorry. I guess I'm just a little nervous. The assignment and being in a strange place. I'm not usually so squeamish, but I have low tolerance for bugs."

"*No* tolerance is more like it." He grinned as he climbed out of the truck and walked around to let her out.

By the time he got to her door, she'd already climbed down. Her independence twisted around his sense of chivalry, threatening to choke it. He'd been taught at an early age that women expected certain things of a man. Opening doors sat high on the list. He still felt like a heel for not helping her at the bar. When she reached for the suitcase in the truck bed, he stopped her with his best 'back off' look.

"Don't you ever get tired of being Ms. Independence? I'd think after the night you've had you'd be glad to have somebody take care of you."

Her sidelong glance told him he'd hit a nerve.

"I don't need to be taken care of. I've been on my own for a very long time and I've done perfectly fine."

"Well, you've obviously never been through anything like this before. When I walked into your hotel room, you were on the edge."

"I told you I don't like bugs. That's all."

Three

Her tone sounded a little too indignant to be believed and he considered calling her on it, but when he saw the soft glow of her skin go pale, he let it go. He looked down to see what had caught her attention. She stood staring at the dead flower sticking out of her suitcase. It must have got caught up in the clothes when he'd stuffed them inside. All the better, he thought. He could have it analyzed to make sure it didn't have any poisons or anything like that on it.

"Let's go inside and we'll talk about it."

She quietly followed him into the house. He watched her carefully as her gaze shifted from the black lacquer dining room set to the white leather sofa in the living room. Her attention finally settled on the one-hundred-gallon fish tank occupying the far wall of the dining room. Paul felt a sense of self-satisfaction at the expression on her face. He'd purposely set the tank in that position, making it visible from any point in the main rooms of the house.

"It's spectacular, isn't it?" He didn't even try to hide his pride. Life as a news reporter could be damn lonely at times and fish are low maintenance pets. The saltwater tank has proved to be a vital stress reliever and a great conversation starter. He couldn't even count how many times he'd been on deadline and blocked. He'd set his laptop at the far end of the table and let the sight of the tank ease him through his crisis.

"Did you put it together yourself?" Maggie walked over and peered into the tank.

Paul moved beside her. "I set every piece of coral and plant life just where I thought the little guys would like them." He smiled when she threw him a questioning look. "It's their home, what good would it be if they weren't comfortable?"

The sound of her laughter echoed in the room. It'd been a long time since anybody had laughed in his house. He would never have imagined it to be her. Their gazes met and Paul swore the current between them had enough strength to carry him away. He forced his hands to remain at his sides. He had no right to know what her tawny brown hair felt like. But the memory of holding her in her room haunted him. He had even less right to know what her full cinnamon-colored lips tasted like.

"I'll take your bags up to the extra room."

"I'm surprised you have extra rooms. Do you live here alone?" She walked around the table and wandered into the living room. He picked up her bags and followed.

"I do now. There are four bedrooms. This used to be my parent–mother's house, but she moved back to Kenner several years ago. My brothers and I shared it for a while, but they all went their own ways. So, I bought out their shares.

"How many brothers do you have? If I'm not being too personal."

He watched her hand slide along the marble fireplace and imagined how it would feel on his chest.

"I'm sorry; I didn't mean to pry."

Paul realized he'd been staring and that she'd asked him a question. "No, it's fine. I have three. One younger and two older."

"Wait a minute. The man in the bar, he called you little brother. Didn't he?"

Paul nodded. "Yep. Holt is the second son. He owns Chaser's. That's one of the reasons he moved out of here. He lives above the bar now."

"Nice place. Although I have to admit, it would have been more pleasant if I'd not run into–"

"Me?" Even though he had definite opinions about women and things, he should know better than to shoot off his mouth in front of strangers, especially females.

"Well, since you said it. Do you really believe all that crap you were going on about earlier?"

Paul considered how to answer, he decided not to. He was tired, so he knew she must be exhausted. "I'll show you to your room so you can get some sleep." He stopped at the bottom of the staircase when she didn't follow. "Is there a problem?"

"Yes." Maggie folded her arms across her chest.

"What?"

"You."

His eyebrow shot up. "Why?" Paul was getting incredibly bored with their single syllabic conversation. He decided to liven things up by jumping from the frying pan into the fire. "Pray tell, what have I done to offend you this time?"

"I asked you a question earlier and you didn't answer me."

Paul thought for a minute, realizing there might have been several. "Which one?"

"I want to know what the card said."

Direct hit. This one didn't beat around the bush, and she didn't give up. After setting her bag down on the carpet, he led her to the sofa. Before he sat, he pulled off his coat. Once she'd joined him. He reached into his pocket and pulled out the small square of paper. She tried to grab it away, but he held it out of her reach. "I'll read it."

"Fine. Today please."

"*Headline: Reporter Exterminated! Go home and don't bug us.*" "Oh my God. What in the name of he-heaven is that supposed to mean?"

"Are you joking, or could you possibly be so dense?"

Maggie stood, nearly tipping his coffee table over. Several small candles toppled to the floor. She scurried around the table, picking up the rolling distractions. He imagined her mind racing with sharp retorts. The dazed look vanished when she opened her mouth.

"Just a dang minute. What right do you have to talk to me like that?"

Karen L. Syed

"Look, Maggie. I was under the impression you knew what you were doing. You came here to do a story on organized crime in a small town. Did you think you would go unnoticed?"

"I figured the paper would be the only one to know I was here."

She took the hit as reality dealt her ego a cruel blow and she sat back down. Paul almost felt bad for her.

"Why would I figure that? I am dealing with the mob."

Paul shook his head. "This may be a small town, but not everybody in it has a small town IQ. We get a lot of mob activity from the low men in the business wanting to work their way up in the ranks. This is serious business and they mean what they say."

"You sound like you know from personal experience." She looked at him curiously.

He rolled up the sleeve of his shirt and held his elbow out toward her. She flinched at the sight. A hideous black and purple bruise covered most of his arm. "This is courtesy of the Greely brothers."

"Why'd they do it?" Maggie reached out.

He forced himself not to pull back as she stroked her fingertips across the tender flesh. A shadow of her touch remained after she'd moved away. The lingering sensation of her caress left him nearly panting. Thoughts of the Greelys quelled his racing heart.

"I stuck my head in an office door at the courthouse where Packston was doing some business.

They wanted to teach me a lesson about knocking before opening a door." Paul rolled his sleeve back down, but didn't button it.

"So, what was he doing?"

Ah, he thought. The reporter surfaces. "As far as I can figure, he was getting a marriage license. What I don't know, is why it's such a big secret."

"So, who is Packston Greely marrying? And why would anyone want to be with a gangster?"

"The only thing I could find out when I asked questions is that she's local." He watched Maggie look around the room. "You lose something?"

"My bag. I have some notes about a connection I found."

Paul went to get her briefcase. After several minutes of digging, she pulled out a file folder. He waited while she shuffled through the stack of computer printed pages. She glanced over several, put the folder away, and stood.

"Are you going to share with me?" Paul hadn't got a good look at any of the pages.

"I hadn't planned on it. Why would I?" She paused. "I'm really very tired."

"I wish you would try to trust me."

Maggie barked out a laugh. "Trust you?" She stood still for a moment, and then began pacing the room. "I don't even know you. Why would I trust a man I don't even know?"

Somebody had hurt her. Paul could see it written all over her face.

"I'm going to bed."

"Maggie, I didn't mean to upset you. It has nothing to do with my male ego." He stared at her. "That *is* what you're thinking, isn't it? I mean it seems to be your generic answer for everything. If you don't think it's right or fair, it's just some man trying to shove his ego down your throat."

"Not only is that not true, but it's downright mean to say." Her lip trembled, but she held back the tears pooling in her eyes.

She'd pegged his self-centered, chauvinist tendencies. He knew it and so did Maggie. That didn't mean he had to like it. "And…" he began.

"Sometimes the truth hurts. The sooner you accept your shortcomings, the better off you'll be."

Paul held her stare. "Am I being charged for this session, Doctor?"

"I'm just stating the obvious." Maggie stood her ground.

"You know, *chère*, you would be a beautiful woman if you spent less time with your face screwed up looking like you could snap the world in half."

Fire sparked in Maggie's eyes like a splash of molten lava. She moved toward Paul until he could feel the heat of her body reaching out to caress him. His gaze stayed locked with hers, his breathing grew raspy, and he saw a flash of something different in her eyes. Fear?

"Take me to my room," she hissed.

"Come again, *chère*."

"Don't be ridiculous. I'm tired. Besides, there's nothing you can do for me up there." Maggie turned, heading for the stairs.

"You know, it must take a lot out of a person to be this way all the time. And don't underestimate what I can do . . ." Paul stepped past her and headed up the stairs with her bag. He heard her huffing and puffing at the bottom of the stairs and he smiled.

"You are a pompous fool," Maggie snapped.

"You are a bra burning pain in the butt." He paused briefly and waited for a retort. The air grew still, similar to what happens just before a storm erupts. Then she surprised him.

"Thanks for letting me stay here."

Paul barely heard her comment. "You're welcome. I'm sorry about the welcome committee's gift." He opened the bedroom door and dropped the bag inside the room. "The bathroom is across the hall and right now it's the only one working. We'll have to share. I'll see you in the morning."

He closed her door and walked into his own room. When he looked at the king-sized sleigh bed, Paul realized its immense size for the first time. It'd been his first reward to himself after getting hired on as a full-time investigator for the Port Ray Reporter. He calculated in his mind, only six more payments and it would be his. Another revelation came at him as he stared at the bed. The only person who'd ever slept in it, was him. *Some stud I am.*

* * *

Across the hall, Maggie sat on the edge of the bed trying to remember how long it had been since she'd slept in a house with a man. She'd lived with one of her boyfriends for almost a month before he'd kicked her out. He didn't take kindly to having a live-in girlfriend cursed with being the only twenty-one-year-old virgin left on earth. Even her heartfelt declaration of love hadn't stopped him from shoving her out the door, but not before he got what he wanted. Had really been five years already? Since then, she'd gotten used to sleeping alone. *So I'm not a sexual goddess.*

"Stop it! Get them off me!"

Paul ran into Maggie's room without knocking. He stopped cold when he saw her thrashing around on her bed. The down comforter lay in a heap on the floor at the foot of the bed. He watched Maggie struggling to get free of the sheets tangled around her legs. "Maggie. It's me, Paul. You're fine."

Her eyes, open wide, shone eerily with intense terror, but Paul knew she wasn't fully awake. Her usually bright green eyes glistened with tears.

"Get them off me. I can't stand it." She swatted at her arms while struggling against the pull of the plaid sheets. "Make it stop, Paul. Please." Her nails dug into her skin as she clawed and scratched until long red welts blazed across her ivory flesh.

"There's nothing on you, *chère*, You're just having a bad dream. Look." He held her hands in his, turning them over so she could see both sides.

Maggie blinked several times then stared blindly at her arms. Her body trembled and tears streamed down her cheeks. "No, I can feel them. They're all over me."

"No, *chère* , I promise, there's nothing on you. I wouldn't let anything hurt you."

Wrapping his arms around her, he felt her relax. "That's it. Just relax."

Without warning, her body began to tremble. Uncontrollable sobs shook them both. Finally, she went limp in his arms.

"It seemed so real."

Without letting her go, Paul pulled the sheet up and made sure there were no unwelcome visitors in her bed. He noticed his own hand trembling slightly.

"I can't believe I'm being such a baby about this." In a gesture more charming than it should have been, Maggie swiped her arm across her face and sniffled.

"Shh, you're all right."

Paul gathered her against him and she let him pull her closer. "I'm sorry."

For the second time in one night, Maggie found herself in Paul's arms. How could this be happening? She couldn't be finding comfort with someone like him. She didn't even like him. The crawling sensation on her skin lessened. She allowed the strength of his embrace to ease her panic. A sigh escaped her lips.

The rubbing of his hand up and down the length of her arms started a new kind of tingling. Noticing his hands, she thought them much too large to be so gentle. A man's hands, rough, but neatly kept. His thumb rubbed in small soothing circles. Maggie relaxed against him.

"Why are you so afraid of bugs?" Paul hesitated. "I mean, I've seen fear, but yours comes closer to terror."

His question startled her. The familiar panic began rising and fought against the mental pictures forming in her mind. She couldn't go through it again. The damp walls of her aunt's cellar, the musty smell, and— the bugs. Small bugs she couldn't see, crawling along her exposed skin. Her throat tightened, strangling a scream. It didn't matter; nobody would hear her. She'd screamed before and nobody heard.

Maggie remembered pounding on the door, begging her parents to hear her. She'd gone down to get her special gift for her father before he left on his next trip. She'd been so angry with her parents for leaving her behind. They left thinking she was still angry. Then they'd died. She'd never been able to tell them how much she loved them.

"Maggie, calm down. I'm right here."

He rocked her back and forth. She turned her head up so she could look at him. Looking into his eyes, she wondered, where the chips of ice she'd seen earlier had gone. Gazing up at him now, she saw only warmth and concern. "You heard." She heard her own voice.

"I heard you cry out, I came as fast as I could."

He didn't understand what she meant, but she was

too tired to explain. He'd probably think she was being foolish anyway.

"I'm sorry I woke you up. I hardly ever have bad dreams anymore." *Damn, why'd you say that*? She looked up at him and waited for him to question her, but he remained silent. She'd never told anyone about the nightmares before. No one knew she'd ever had them, until now. His arms loosened and she felt him tugging away.

"I'll let you go back to sleep. I have an early appointment."

He started to get up, but Maggie couldn't let him. She stiffened herself, but held fast to his arm. "Not that it's a big deal, but could you stay a little longer? I mean if you'd rather not, I'll understand."

He looked down at her, his features soft and more sympathetic than she liked. She hated the pity she knew he felt, but she needed the comfort he offered with it. It had been too long since she'd felt this way in a man's arms. In fact she'd never felt this way. She wanted to enjoy it for a little longer before she put an end to it.

Once the sun came up it would be back to work. She had a job to do; now it seemed someone didn't want her to do it. She'd get the story; then she'd make them sorry they'd ever threatened her. She silently vowed it would take more than a few—a shiver ran the length of her spine—bugs to scare her off.

"I'll stay, but only if you're sure." Even before she answered he lay down again.

Before she had a chance to settle thoroughly, he shifted his legs up onto the bed. She handed him a pillow. He fluffed it up then stuffed it behind his back. When they'd both found comfortable positions, she rested her head against his shoulder. Reaching for the covers, she felt the strap of her nightie fall off her shoulder. He reached up and slid it back into place. The tips of his fingers brushed lightly against her bare flesh. The sensation of something wild made her tremble. Her breath caught when his hand lingered.

His heart raced against the palm of her hand, and it unsettled her. The soft mat of hair on his chest padded the thumping. She forced her thoughts in a different direction. Counting each beat, she lost track of time and slipped off to sleep.

Paul held himself perfectly still beneath her. He'd almost lost it when her strap had slid down. He stared down at the thin strip of material and the flawless skin it rested on. Smooth and tempting. Too tempting. How could someone so hard, look so soft? Feel so soft? She worked so hard at being a rock, but here she lay, asleep in his arms, still shaking. As soft and vulnerable as anyone he'd ever seen. Night and day.

That's what she was. No, he thought. *Fire and ice.* Well, whatever, she had the most exasperating way of getting his dander up. His mind skipped back to the comment about nightmares, he made a mental note to ask her about it at a more appropriate time. As annoying as she could be, he didn't like the idea of anything or anyone frightening her.

Since he couldn't get to sleep, he tried piecing together what had happened in her hotel room. The dead flowers and bugs was a childish prank, but very effective. Even so, they'd known exactly what to do to get to her. They must have somehow gotten a profile on her. Psychological warfare? The thought of someone playing games with Maggie's mind set him on edge. Some of the air puffed out of his overinflated ego when he remembered his own plan. He'd decided to do the same thing. Scare her out of town so he could have his own story. But that was different. Wasn't it?

Pushing aside his own guilt, he silently speculated on the obvious culprit in this game. If he had to make bet on it, he'd put his money on Packston. Norbert and Alvin were henchmen. They didn't have the brains between them to pull of something like this. They'd probably done the legwork, but he'd definitely credit Packston as the brains behind it. Perhaps in the morning, he'd pay the slug a visit. He'd never let Packston hurt Maggie.

Even in sleep, Maggie remained agitated and restless. It wasn't until her breathing evened out, Paul allowed himself to relax. He made sure he didn't let himself rub against her any more than he had to. He closed his eyes and breathed in. The balsam scent of her hair pulled the burning knot in his stomach tighter as the heat raced to lower regions. After an hour of lying with her, he found himself still rubbing her arm. Her skin felt like satin against his. How could something so smooth and delicate have such a powerful effect on him?

He lay awake, imagining her waiting at the door for him when he got home from work. He could almost smell the pot roast in the kitchen cooking. When he finally fell asleep, Maggie filled his dreams. Only she wasn't waiting for him at home. She stayed by his side as they skulked in the shadows of an alley. Alive, full of life and enthusiasm, they worked side by side.

When he woke up, a sheen of perspiration covered his skin, and he had a pain only one thing would cure. Knowing he couldn't have that, he decided to go to plan B.

Paul slipped out of her warm embrace and hurried to the bathroom. He turned the knob on the faucet letting the freezing water pour out full force. He stepped into the claw-foot tub and pulled the plastic curtain around. Water rushed over him, easing the physical discomfort with a different kind of pain, but did little to alleviate the stress on his emotional state. He had to face facts. One, Maggie Howell had been sent to work with him–bad. Two, he wanted her–also bad. Lastly, he would probably never have her–the worst. He'd just have to stay away from her during her stay. He heard her knock as he stepped out of the shower. "I'll be right out."

"I just wanted to let you know I made some coffee and breakfast will be ready in a few minutes."

But not too far away. Paul smiled in spite of himself. It would be nice to eat something he hadn't had to cook himself.

He pulled his robe around himself and stepped out into the hall. She looked radiant standing in her bedroom doorway. The earth-tone-colored robe accented her tawny skin. He felt the tightening return. Twenty minutes in the freezing shower ran straight down the drain. Turning away, he walked into his own room, slamming the door behind him.

"Are you always so chipper in the morning?" She sounded like she was standing right outside his door.

The thought of her being so close shook him. "You can go ahead. I'll be down in a minute."

Maggie stared at the closed door for several minutes before heading down the stairs. She didn't know how long she'd lain awake this morning before Paul left her room. She felt her cheeks flush when she thought about how she'd acted like a baby. Ms. Independence, my foot.

She trailed her hand along the built-in shelf as she went down the stairs. Most of it remained empty. A few of the shelves however, held pictures of people she didn't know. Of course she didn't know them. Why should I, she thought? I don't belong here. I don't belong anywhere. She stopped next to a large framed photo of Paul's family, or so she assumed. She recognized Holt standing behind Paul. She stared at the woman in the middle of the four boys. She sat tall with her shoulders squared. She had warm gray eyes that matched her glowing smile. The picture reminded

Maggie of what she'd missed in life.

She was the only child born to Maxwell and Margaret Howell. Not by choice. An infection after Maggie's birth had left her mother unable to have any more children. So, in a sense, Maggie figured she had no one to blame but herself.

For years she'd been the sole object of her parent's attention, until her father got his new job. Being a truck driver kept him away for weeks at a time. Over the months, her mother had grown lonely and sullen. Maggie remembered when her father was home, he'd lavished her with gifts, but there were few gifts for her mother. Margaret had never worked. Even when her husband went on the road she stayed at home making sure she had dinner on the table every night just in case he'd surprise them. He never did.

One week after her fourteenth birthday, her parents had died. Her father had come home with a new rig and had insisted her mother go for a ride in it with him. The cab flipped on a mountain road killing them both. All the fights had always made her wonder if her parents would stay together. Maggie felt little comfort in knowing they had stayed together to the very end.

Maggie had loved her mother. She'd been a good woman with so much to offer. Maggie had inherited few of her mother's domestic skills, but she could cook if it meant the difference between starving or not. She knew how to operate a washing machine and she knew to dust before the furniture disappeared. Other than that, she was green to say the least. Being a reporter, she'd learned the joys of eating out and to having someone come in twice week to give the place the once over.

I'll bet he has a maid come in every day, she thought. Irritated that she even cared, she stood on her tiptoes and searched for dust back in the corner of the shelf. She heard Paul's door squeak open and crept down the stairs.

She hoped she hadn't got his hopes up when she said breakfast would be ready. She remembered the waffles in the microwave and dashed down the remaining few stairs. When she opened the microwave door, her shoulders sagged. They didn't look very appetizing and when she poked them with her finger, the density confirmed her assessment. They weren't going to taste very good either. Maybe some syrup would help.

Four

She set two plates on the black lacquer table and poured coffee into both cups. She pulled the newspaper out of the plastic bag and sat at the far end of the table. She left the opposite end open for Paul so he could face his aquarium. When he came into the dining room, he smiled.

"You really did cook. I thought I might have been dreaming." He looked over at her when he realized what he'd said. She pretended she hadn't heard him.

Maggie watched him. He wore a bright smile, up until the second he tried to cut his waffle. The knife jerked off the waffle and grated across the plate, they both cringed. She rubbed her jaw hoping the peculiar grinding feeling would disappear soon. Paul struggled to cut the square on his plate. Finally, a piece separated from the rest. He looked at her hesitantly, then shoved it into his mouth.

"Mmm, dis is–beyond words." He chewed forever before he finally gulped down the food. Maggie had to give him credit. She'd almost decided not to eat hers.

"Thank you. I can't cook too many things, but I figured I couldn't mess these up too bad."

He nodded, and then swallowed another bite. "Eat up. You had a rough night and you need your strength." Maggie couldn't tell if it was genuine concern or revenge making him say the words. In any case, it didn't really matter. If he could eat the waffles, so could she.

Breakfast took longer than it should have, but Maggie stayed until the bitter end. When she put the last bite in her mouth, Paul stood up and carried the dirty dishes into the kitchen. Maggie contemplated helping him wash them, but was saved from that horrible fate when he appeared in the dining room only minutes later.

"I think, if you don't mind, you should stay around the house today. I don't want anyone finding you alone."

The relaxed atmosphere crashed around her and Maggie glowered at him. "I most certainly do mind. I came here to do a job and I intend to get it done, so I can go home."

"Maggie, be reasonable. Obviously, someone doesn't want you doing this. Why don't you just cut your losses before you get hurt?" He stood looking down at her with his arms folded over his chest. He looked more like a father than she cared for.

"I am quite capable of taking care of myself. Thank you for your concern. Now if you'll excuse me." She stood to walk away, but he caught her arm.

"Maggie. The Greelys may seem like small time hoods on the surface, but they can make a hell of a mess when they put their minds to it. I don't want you getting caught in the crossfire of all this." His voice softened and Maggie almost gave in. "Just let me handle this."

"What?" she bellowed. "Let you handle this? Handle what? Me?" She shook herself loose from his grasp and stepped away. "Or maybe let you handle the story, so you can get full credit for it."

"What are you getting so mad about? I'll tell you what I find out, and then you can write your story from my notes."

Maggie took a step forward and leaned in as close to his face as she could without touching him. "You listen to me, buster. I'll get my own story, and I'll do it without your help. I am not some prissy fluff writer who needs you to hold my hand."

His previous words came flying back at him. She smiled when he backed down. Her barb regarding his earlier comment hit home and she dug her heel into it–hard.

"I don't need some *big strong man* to do what I am quite capable of doing myself. I've done stories a heck of a lot riskier than this one, and I'm here to tell about it. So, if you'll get out of my way, I need to get dressed."

Paul stared at her, then stepped back. Maggie stood at the bottom of the stairs before she realized he'd followed her. "Maggie. I know what I said yesterday was stupid. I'm sorry, but I really don't want anything to happen to you. I'll give you my cell phone number in case you need me.

Maggie took the first step, ~~then~~ and turned to face him. The warmth of his breath so close to her face startled her. She had to reform her thought. Tilting her head back, she stared at him for a brief, tenderly agonizing moment. His concern for her was more than she could comprehend. As much as she longed for someone to care, she wasn't sure if she wanted it to be him. No matter how enticing he looked.

"Are you okay, Maggie?"

She nodded and pulled up the walls of her emotional defenses. "I appreciate you helping me out last night and for letting me stay here. I'm sorry if I caused you any inconvenience." The sarcasm in her voice made her stomach churn. It's the only way, she told herself.

"You didn't."

"I'll look into one of the boarding houses and be out by tonight." She left him standing at the bottom of the stairs with his mouth hanging open. She hadn't expected him to look disappointed. He should be glad to be rid of her. Why wasn't she glad to be going?

Paul watched her stomp up the stairs. Her robe flapping behind her gave him much too clear a view of her tanned legs. He hadn't meant to offend her. He hadn't even meant to talk to her. When he'd come downstairs he was going to get his bag and go to the office. The nice quiet office where he could get a cup of coffee, a donut, and her off his mind.

Now, here he was, standing in his own home feeling like a complete jerk with lead waffles weighing down his stomach. *The good news is she's leaving.* The small voice inside his head continued, *And why is that good news?* He ignored the voice

The sooner she left, the sooner he could get his mind back on his job. Hal wanted a story on his desk in two weeks and he still had his regular column to do. He had plenty of work to keep him busy. He went into the study and sat down to make a list.

1. Call florist.

Paul wondered what Maggie's favorite flower was. He'd bet the farm it wasn't orchids. At least not anymore.

2. Read Maggie's earlier articles on organized crime.

Again his thoughts strayed to Maggie. Had she been in danger when she'd investigated those other stories? Had someone else out there protected her then?

He leaned back in his chair and stared out the window. The bay window allowed him an excellent view of the man-made lake behind his house. Morning mist drifted softly down, landing on the glass. The heat inside the house gave indication of how hot it was outside. He decided that once he wrote the Greely story he'd take his vacation and go do some skiing. He thought of how cold Maggie had turned when he'd suggested he cover the story. He closed his eyes and pictured Maggie swishing down the slopes with her sandy brown hair flowing from under her goggle strap. Even in a snowsuit she looked hot. Not hot enough. Maybe he'd go water skiing. In Bermuda.

"I called a cab and I'll be leaving as soon as he gets here."

Paul's eyes snapped open. He turned around and opened his mouth to say something. He closed it again when the words slipped away. She wore a pair of navy blue leggings she had to have painted on. The thin peach sweater she wore hung down just above the ridges of her well-muscled thighs. She'd pulled her hair back in a tight ponytail accenting her strong jaw lines. Her cheeks glowed pink. He wondered if she'd put on makeup or if she glowed naturally. Either way, she looked delicious.

"I've been thinking about it, and I'd like it if you'd stay here." The words spewed out before he'd even realized he'd been thinking them.

"Why?"

"I have plenty of room and-"

"And what?" Maggie persisted.

"I'd just like it."

She sat on the sofa against the far wall. She inspected her fingernails, brushed a speck of lint of her dark pants, and scratched her chin. "There have to be some ground rules."

"Hold on. This is my house," he argued.

She stood up. "Fine, I'll be out of here shortly."

"All right. What?" He leaned back and listened to the rumble of her voice. Smooth alto, with a hint of softness.

"I come and go as I please and I am not required to share any information I get with you."

"You can come and go as you please, if you leave a note, and you'll exchange me item for item."

"Humph!" She stood up and walked to the door. "Fine, but I won't cook."

Paul smiled as she walked out of the room. "Thank God."

Her laughter carried through the house as she ascended the stairs.

"And cancel the cab; I'll take you to your car." *That's showin' her, bub.* Never let the woman get the last word, he thought.

"I never called."

He laughed.

Half an hour later, Maggie watched Paul drive away. Thankful for the time alone, she stood next to her car. She lifted her head, letting the morning rays beat down on her face. A slight breeze took away some of the sun's intensity.

Bits of her earlier conversation with Paul swam around in her head. He'd lived in Port Ray his entire life. His words came back to her. Dangerous. Sick. Vicious. She seriously considered the possibility she might have underestimated the power of small-time hoods.

"Well, Ms. Howell, how nice to see you out and about."

Maggie turned to see who the strange voice

belonged to. She looked up into what she could only describe as devilishly brown eyes. There was nothing sensual or passionate about them. They held a glint of menace. She immediately sensed his evil. Her skin crawled and the heat of his gaze burned straight through her soul.

"I'm sorry. I don't believe we've met." Maggie took a cautious step back, but he moved with her. He shoved his hands deep into the pockets of his leather coat. His stance was self-assured and arrogant. She knew exactly who he was. She'd seen more than enough photos of him and his family.

"Not formally, but I feel as if I know you." His gaze slipped down the length of her body. She shivered.

"I was so sorry to learn about your parent's death. It must have been horrible for you."

Her skin crawled at the thought of a complete stranger knowing about a loss so personal, and so long ago. "My parents died quite a few years ago. How did you know?" she mumbled.

"Did they ever prove the brake lines were faulty? No, of course they didn't. They closed it off as an accident."

Maggie remembered there had been an investigation, but her aunt had assured her it was an accident. How could this stranger know about it?

As if he'd read her mind he answered her questions. "My name is Packston Greely. What a terrible loss it must have been."

Her insides churned and she prayed with all her might that if she did get sick it would be on his feet. The very idea that her father could know someone like the Greelys bothered her. But then the man in front of her was no more than a year or two older than her. How could he know so much? "Is there something I can do for you, Mr. Greely?" The name tasted vile on her tongue. In her mind, she vowed to find every piece of dirt she could on his family.

"I would think under the circumstances, you would be eager to go home. I really don't think there is anything here for you." He brushed the lapel of his flannel suit peeking from inside the expensive jacket. "There's a bus leaving at noon. No one would be the slightest bit unhappy if you were on it."

"I guess you'll have to be disappointed then, because I won't be on it. I think I'll be staying on for longer than I'd planned."

His lip curled as he leaned toward her. The smell of stale cigarette smoke on his breath nearly gagged her. He raised his hand, again fingering the lapel of his hideously pinstriped suit. "I'm sorry to hear that. I thought we could reach an agreeable understanding."

"Get over it," Maggie spat at him. She walked around to the driver's door and climbed into the car. She glanced in her rearview mirror. Pulling away from the curb, she glanced back. Packston Greely stood in the middle of the road glaring after her.

She drove down several streets until she found the county library. After she'd parked the car, she leaned her forehead on the steering wheel. Her heart pounded in her ears like the drums of an old Congo Square. Driving usually helped her remain calm, but the intense fear gripping her remained this time. Packston Greely was a seriously evil man. It showed in his smile. It gleamed in his eyes. And it echoed in his voice. She'd have to be very careful of him.

She noticed few people in the library when she walked in. A petite, elderly woman sat at a table stacked with magazines. As Maggie walked by, she noticed the woman was copying recipes. The only other person in the room looked to be the same age as her. The woman sat curled up on an antique looking sofa, reading a romance novel. Maggie set her bag on the table nearest her and pulled out a chair. The wooden legs scraped against the hardwood floors and the woman looked up. Struck immediately by the sadness in the woman's eyes, Maggie forced a smiled. The woman lowered her eyes and went back to her reading.

Pulling out her tablet, Maggie headed to the periodical files on the far end of the room. More than once, she looked up to find the woman staring at her. When she'd collected all the back issues of the local newspapers she could carry, she returned to her table. Quietly, she scanned the sheets looking for any references to the Greely family. She found several incidents involving the three Greely brothers and more than a few of them involved one of the Remington brothers. According to the Port Ray Reporter there was no love lost between the two families. There were even a few editorials speculating on age-old voodoo curses put on the Remington family by past Greelys.

Maggie pulled up a paper from only a month earlier. She was nearly finished when she caught a glimpse of a familiar face. Maggie read the engagement announcement, then glanced over at her neighbor. The newspaper picture didn't do her nearly enough justice. Maggie read the article. *Local Businessman's Daughter to Marry Packston Greely*. Maggie shuddered. What would possess a father to let something like that happen? Then her reporter instincts kicked in. She had an idea. After refolding the newspapers, she returned them to the marred wooden file cabinet.

"Hi. My name is Maggie Howell." Maggie held her hand out, but the other woman only stared at her. "Can I join you?"

"Well, actually I am trying to finish this before I have to leave."

"Is it a good one? You know I read romances sometimes when I need to relax."

"I'm Francesca." Her answer was short and curt. Maggie considered walking away, but she'd never been able to pass up a challenge.

"I'm new in town and I seem to be a little short on friends."

Francesca put her book down and looked up at Maggie. "Isn't that funny, I've lived here all my life and I'm also short of friends."

Taking the hint, Maggie stepped back. "Sorry I bothered you. I'll be going now." She'd have to find another way to dredge up information on Packston.

"Wait."

Maggie stopped.

"I'm sorry. I didn't mean to be rude. I've just had a rough week and I'm not used to people being nice to me."

Maggie saw something flash in her eyes. She recognized the distant hurt lingering just beneath the surface. She knew the hurt; she felt it every day. "Well, maybe a new friend is just what we both need."

"Maybe. Are you planning on staying or just passing through?" Francesca set her book down on her leg. She looked around the room as if looking for someone.

"I'm not sure," Maggie lied. "Have you lived here all your life?"

Francesca smiled weakly. "Every dreadful day."

"You don't like it here?" Maggie asked. Her new friend shifted in her seat and lowered her eyes. "I'm sorry. Am I prying?"

"No. It's not that. I'm just not used to talking about myself."

"That's okay. I don't like talking about myself either. What would you like to talk about?" Maggie wanted to ask her about her relationship with Packston, but didn't want to scare the skittish woman off.

"Where are you from?"

Maggie considered lying, but opted to go the easy

route. "I'm from a town just north of Shreveport. I got in last night."

"You alone, or are you with your husband?" Maggie had to give the woman credit; she'd make a great reporter. She was the only one getting any answers.

"I'm alone. I was staying at the hotel, but now I'll be staying with a friend."

"You're not married?" Francesca's brow went up.

Finally, a lead in. "No, life as a reporter doesn't leave much room for romance."

"You're a reporter?"

"Guilty as charged." Maggie half expected her new friend to tell her to bug off, but she didn't.

"Are you working on a story, or is this a pleasure trip?"

"Hey, I thought I was the reporter. You're asking all the questions." When the woman's smile slipped, Maggie laughed, trying to ease her nervousness. "It's all right. It's actually kinda nice being on this end for a change. At least now I know what it feels like."

"You never answered my question."

"What's that?"

"Are you here on business or pleasure?"

Maggie had a feeling she could trust Francesca Raynor. Going with her instincts, she dove right in to finish what she'd started. "Business, I was sent here to investigate the implications of organized crime in your town." Maggie reached out for Francesca's hand when her face paled. "Are you all right?" Francesca's hand trembled under hers. Maggie knew she'd pegged Packston right.

"I just got engaged to be married." She paused before she went on. "To Packston Greely."

Maggie sensed the hesitancy in Francesca and wondered if she knew what the Greelys were up to. She seemed like a nice enough girl, but not really the strong type.

Francesca went on. "I'm not sure if it will actually happen." Francesca pulled her hand away.

"Don't you love him?"

"No. My father arranged it all. I mean, Packston's handsome in a strange kind of way, but I don't think he's my kind of man."

Relieved by the woman's answer, Maggie thought very carefully before she spoke again. "So, do you have to marry him? Can't you explain to your father that there just aren't any sparks?"

Francesca's laugh sounded soft and hollow. Its sadness sent chills down Maggie's spine.

"Packston has worked for my father for some time, and in my father's life, business is everything. I only know of one thing more important to my father than his business; his wife."

"Your mother? Don't you get along?"

Francesca leaned forward and Maggie saw the hurt in her eyes deepen. "Natalie is not my mother. My mother is dead."

Maggie was about to ask another question when the library door slammed open. Standing in the entryway with the sun casting rays around him, was Packston Greely. His cocky grin said more than a thousand words. Francesca scrambled off the sofa. Maggie caught her hand before she could get away. "It was nice talking to you. I hope we can do it again. Soon."

Francesca looked at Packston who swaggered toward them. "That would be nice. Really nice."

Maggie watched as Packston threw his arm around Francesca. Maggie didn't think he'd seen her. She breathed a sigh of relief, grateful for the wood columns placed around the room. She'd been able to look around it while remaining hidden. It gave her a chance to watch the unlikely couple.

"I didn't mean to make you wait, Packston."

"Well, it's not the first time." He reached down and smacked her on the bottom.

Francesca scooted forward in an effort to avoid any further contact.

"Why do you always do that?" Packston stared down at her.

"Do what?" She asked, feigning innocence. The very thought of him touching her made her physically sick. The farther away from him she stayed, the better.

"Good Lord. I don't know what the big deal is. We're damn near married. I think I've earned a little bit of a sample of what I'm getting."

From somewhere deep inside her Francesca pulled up a wisp of courage. "You're getting a wife. A very rich wife."

"So, for this I have to live with a cold fish?" He pulled her up against him and leaned down to assault her lips with his.

His tongue slipped between her lips and she struggled against the burning in her throat. What little food she'd had for lunch slowly rose upward, the bitter taste of his foul breath choking her. Worse than his physical invasion was the knowledge of others watching him mark his territory. She knew she was no longer Francesca Raynor. She was Packston Greely's woman.

She slumped against him in emotional defeat. *Will I ever be my own person?*

Five

Paul stood outside the Duncan's Florist Shop. He tried to remember how many times he'd been by the shop. Then he tried to remember the last time he'd bought a woman–other than his mother–flowers. It took a special woman to move him to the point of that kind of thing. Hmm, he wondered. Pondering the situation, he decided Maggie was most definitely an orchid kind of girl. Or at least she was until last night.

The sign said the shop opened at eleven. He looked at his watch; almost quarter after. He had to be in the office by noon, but he needed to find out who'd sent the flowers to Maggie. He was about to go back to his car when an elderly man flipped the closed sign to open and unlocked the door. As he stepped inside the shop, the scent of fresh flowers floated around him. The shop was considerably warmer than the outdoors and he cursed the Louisiana heat.

"Howdy." Flashing a toothless grin, the old man pulled the blinds up. "Sorry 'bout being late. I had to go to the dentist. I broke my biters and had to get fitted for 'dem new ones." The man made a face and pointed to his lack of teeth. "'Taint no fun gettin' old."

Paul shifted restlessly. "Are you the manager?"

"Nope. I own dis here place. Duncan Flavory. Started dis shop for my wife some thirteen years ago. Give us someting to do with retirement." He pointed to a picture on the wall. "She died five years ago, but I couldn't close down. Kept it goin' 'cause I knew dat she'd want me to."

Paul smiled at the sparkle in the man's eyes when he talked about his wife.

The old man stepped behind the counter and closed the cash drawer.

It seemed to Paul the man was in no hurry to take care of him. "I need to ask you some questions."

"'Bout what?"

"Has anyone been in here lately buying dead flowers?" The old man stopped and stared at Paul. "I know that sounds odd, but I really need to know."

"Who wants to know?" the old man snapped.

"My name is Paul Remington. A friend of mine got a delivery from your store last night."

"Don't do no deliveries at night."

"Well they came from your shop."

"How you know dat?"

"The box said so," Paul answered.

"I know not everyone take pride in what dey do, but I don't sell no dead nothin' in dis here shop." He opened a cooler and pulled out a perfect red rose. "Even in dead of summer I can get the best flowers in dis land."

Paul knew he'd offended the man, but he didn't

have time for niceties. "I'm not implying you would. The facts are, a friend of mine received some flowers, and they were in one of your shop's boxes."

"Don't mean they came from here. I don't send no dead flowers to no one."

"Okay, do you remember if anyone ordered flowers to be sent to the Regent hotel?"

The old man pulled out a plastic file box and flipped through the cards. He pulled out a stack and looked through them. "Nothin' to the hotel." He shoved the cards back into the box and closed it. Paul was about to walk away when a stack of receipts caught his attention.

"What are those?" He pointed to the stack on the counter.

"This weekend's receipts. I haven't put dem in the box yet."

"Do you mind if I look through them?" Paul couldn't explain why, but he wasn't ready to let it go. He knew the Greelys were behind the threat. He just needed something to prove it. He'd flipped through most of the stack when he saw Norbert Greely's name. Six orchids had been charged to his account and delivered to the Greely estate.

Paul scribbled down the credit card number while the old man argued about whether it was legal or not. Paul was about to leave when he had an idea. He gave the man his order and scribbled some words on the card. He left specific orders that the flowers be in a vase, not a box.

"Thanks, Mr. Flavory. I'm sorry if I've upset you. You've been a great help."

Paul whistled as he walked to his car. Even after the night he'd had, he still felt like smiling. Waking with Maggie in his arms had scared him to death, but now it didn't seem so bad. Miss Independence had actually cooked him breakfast. It tasted like a hockey puck, but she'd made the effort. Maybe her tough girl armor had some chinks in it, after all.

Maggie walked into the small brick building. A metal desk sat directly in front of the double glass doors. No one sat at the desk. She looked around for signs of life. She found none. Hanging on the wall to the left of the desk were several frames containing certificates. Upon closer inspection she saw several of them had Paul's name inked on them.

There were several awards for outstanding journalism and even some for photography. Her opinion of the small-town reporter increased several times and she made a mental note to compliment him on his achievements.

"I see they rolled out the welcome carpet for you." Paul's voice echoed around her and she turned to face him. He looked larger than life leaning against the doorjamb. The small room shrunk around him.

"I thought you'd already left since I was late." She stepped aside and he walked through a small swinging gate into the back of the office.

"Well, it seems as though punctuality doesn't suit

either of us." He sat at a long folding table and propped his feet on top of it. Maggie would have sworn his legs went on forever if it weren't so obvious where they stopped.

The dark denim hugged his thighs, accenting the taut muscles. The chair creaked under him as he leaned back. She remembered the awards. "You must be really talented."

His smile nearly devastated her composure. Her gaze traveled along the walls of the room. Everywhere but on him. "I mean you must have many talents."

"I like to think so."

Cocky fool. "No. I mean the awards. I saw all the certificates on the wall. Very impressive." Maggie blushed when he raised a brow at her. "I was talking about your writing."

"I know exactly what you were talking about."

A shiver ran the length of her spine when his gaze locked with hers. Something in his expression changed. Maggie decided he had to be the most sensual man she'd ever met. No one had ever looked at her that way and she didn't know how to deal with it.

"Oh." She sat in a chair directly across from him.

"Maggie, we need to talk about something. I don't want you to argue with me, just hear me out." Paul pushed himself up out of the chair. He kept his gaze focused on her as he moved around the table.

"Is this about the story?" She knew he was about to try and convince her to give up on it, but she wouldn't. She'd never quit anything in her life and this story wasn't going to be the first. "You agreed to my demands this morning."

"Maggie, listen. I went to the florist today and found out that Norbert Greely bought the orchids that were left at your door."

Maggie jumped out of the chair. "You got him to admit it?"

"Of course not. He has no idea we know." Paul tugged her back down into her chair.

"Then how do you know it was him?" Maggie asked.

"I saw the credit card receipt and the delivery instructions."

Maggie fell back in her chair. "You saw a piece of paper and this is supposed to convince me." She knew in her heart he was right. Her earlier meeting with Packston reinforced the information. She decided since Paul was already in a mood about the whole situation she would save her information for later. Right now she wanted to see the notes on the Greelys so she could write the opening for her story.

"Maggie. I'm asking you to be careful. I don't want to have to worry about you every time you're out of my sight. I've got a job to do and I can't be digging you out of trouble every ten minutes."

Maggie was on her feet again. "Don't you dare do that. I would have been just fine even if you hadn't come along when you did."

"Yeah? What would you have done? Stand in your room screaming until all the itty-bitty bugs ran away?"

His jab hit hard. Maggie considered slapping him, but it wouldn't make either of them feel better. He was just like every other man she knew. They couldn't let things go and they picked your one weak spot to nail you every time. "Do me a favor and next time I get in trouble, don't do me any favors. I've been on my own for a long time and I've been fine."

"So you've said. I only meant that you don't know what you're dealing with here and I do. If we work together, I'm sure everything will be fine. I don't mind hanging out with you until you're done." His patronizing tone was more than she could stand.

Maggie slammed through the half gate and stopped just on the other side. "Well, I do mind hanging out with you. I don't need, nor do I want your help. I'm getting along just fine." She pushed open the glass door. Before she stepped out, she turned to face him. "By the way I met Packston Greely's fiancé today. Nice girl. Wealth of information." She heard his feet hit the floor just as she stepped out into the blistering afternoon.

The blast of humid air seeped under her skin, promptly extinguishing the fire the arrogant chauvinist had ignited in her. How could somebody with such warm eyes and such a tender smile be such a pig? Maggie smiled. Maybe pig was too harsh a term.

"Maggie, wait." He ran up behind her. "I'm talking to you, damn it. I said wait!"

Maggie dropped her head forward as she kept walking. "Pig!"

"Pig? I'm not a pig," Paul shouted after Maggie as she climbed into her car.

The blast of a truck horn startled him and he realized he was standing in the middle of the road. His frustration at Maggie caused him to react without thinking when the truck driver yelled at him. "Shove that horn up your–"

A burly man crawled down from the truck. "Yeah, well, if you think you're big enough, buddy . . ." He had a good half a foot on Paul, who knew immediately he'd made a rash comment. As the man approached him, Paul considered letting the man put him out of his misery. He decided not to give Maggie Howell the satisfaction.

Paul hurried up onto the sidewalk, backing away from the advancing bear of a man. From the size of him, he figured the man for a lumberjack. Probably knocked trees down by head butting them. "I'm sorry, pal. I didn't think before I spoke. It won't happen again." Paul waved and headed back toward the office. He tried to decide what to do. Should he go home so Maggie could get in the house? Or should he sit right here and wait for her to come looking for him? The whole point of them meeting was so he could give her a key to his house.

Trusting soul, aren't you? That damn voice was back in his head. *You don't know diddly about this girl, except she doesn't make friends well.*

"She's a nice enough sort," he answered himself out loud.

How do you even know she's who she says she is?
"Well, who else would she be?"
Hey, for all you know she may working for Greely.
"Shut up!"

Maggie settled back on Paul's couch. Paul Remington wasn't really that big a deal. Geez, she could go home, wrap Joe around her little finger, and advance her career. But Joe didn't have the ability to set her thighs up in flames by just looking at her. He also didn't have the power to invade her thoughts every time she blinked. Now he thought he could just cast her aside.

Not a chance, Pal!

She'd seen the look in his eyes and even if she wasn't as experienced as some women, she wasn't an idiot.

"I'll show you what happens when you toy with my–hormones." Maggie lay back and went to work on a plan. A plan on how to catch a man. She'd show that male chauvinist that in spite of her independence, she still had the makings of a good woman. She'd give June Cleaver a run for her money. She considered the difference between June and herself. June loved Ward. *I am not in love with Paul.*

Good Lord, I've lost my mind.

A knock on the door saved her from further contemplation. She peeked out the frosted glass to find a deliveryman waiting. Reluctantly, she opened the front door. "Can I help you?"

"I have a delivery for a–Miss Independence."

Maggie burst out laughing when the young boy handed her one dozen red roses, wrapped in clear cellophane and tucked in an oversized clear vase. "Not a bug in sight."

"Excuse me?"

"Nothing." Maggie reached in her jeans pocket and pulled out what little money she had and handed it to the young man.

"No, thank you. It's been taken care of." He smiled and walked away.

Maggie pulled the small card out and read it. *I hope this makes up for your not so warm welcome. Friends? Paul.* Maybe he wasn't so bad after all.

Paul paced the office, shoving his hands through his hair every few steps. Step by step he replayed what had happened. He'd gone up. She'd been there–screaming. Every nerve in his body sparked, causing his muscles to tighten. He sat on the worn couch in his office and clenched his fists. Letting his head fall back against the wall, he counted to ten, ten times. He opened his eyes and looked around the room. When he took a deep breath, he was immediately assailed by the lingering scent of her perfume. Lilacs, she smelled of lilacs. He closed his eyes and started counting again. After counting as high as he knew how, he decided a run would do him good

Forty minutes later, the sweltering heat got the better of him and he slowed his torturous pace. The familiar burn in his chest soothed him and he reveled in the release of it. Moments later, doubt settled in, shattering his calm. The winding road leading to his home loomed behind him and he reconsidered his run. He should just go back to the house and clear the air with Maggie. *Hey, Pal, you already blew it once today. Why not give the lady a break?* He ignored the annoying voice inside his head and kept running. The more he thought about it, the harder he pushed himself, and the worse he felt.

He stayed out long enough to give Maggie time to have gone to sleep. The house was silent, but she'd left the porch light on for him. Maybe she wasn't as mad as he'd thought. He quietly closed up the house, checking all the doors and windows before getting into the shower.

The water streamed down over his body cooling all the places the warm night had touched. Too bad the water couldn't get inside and take away the searing heat Maggie had caused. After pushing his hair back out of his face he leaned his head against the wall. He imagined her standing behind him. He could smell her perfume and almost sense her in the room with him.

Get a grip.

Maggie stood silent, staring at Paul's silhouette through the frosted shower curtain. Even in shadows he looked magnificent. The warm blush of embarrassment crept into her cheeks. She knew she should leave, but the sight of him made it impossible.

Suddenly, his squared shoulders sagged. The gesture of a defeated man. Was she the cause of his frustration? Shaking her head, Maggie hung his robe on the back of the bathroom door. She'd remembered it not being there when she'd taken her shower. He'd be chilled after his shower if he didn't have it. It just wouldn't do for him to get a cold. It would ruin her plans if she had to take care of a sick man.

Closing the door quietly behind her, Maggie went back to her room. She decided to leave her door open a crack. There were already enough walls between them. This would be one less they'd have to get through.

Paul stared at the robe hanging on the hook. He could have sworn he'd left it on his bedroom floor. Obviously not. He pulled it down and burrowed inside it. The oscillating fan hanging on the wall chilled the steamy room, but his robe felt warm. Like someone had just taken it off. Chuckling to himself, he decided he was hanging on the brink of some kind of major breakdown. Once he'd hung his towels up, he tiptoed back to his room. Turning around to close his door, he noticed Maggie's door. She'd left it open.

Damn the woman. She just didn't make sense. One minute she's locking him out, now this. Deciding he didn't want to deal with it now, he crawled into bed. He turned the light off and snuggled under the thin sheet.

"Goodnight, Paul."

He smiled. "Goodnight, Maggie."

* * *

Hours later, Maggie rolled into Paul's arms. His hand cupped her cheek and she relaxed into its warmth. His mouth came toward her slowly. Before she could stop him, he kissed her lightly. First on the forehead, then down on her cheek. Tenderly, his tongue slid along her lower lip, causing her to tremble in his arms. She raised her body closer to him, sighing when he playfully nipped her upper lip. The sucking sensation thrilled her beyond her wildest dreams, making her long for more. He must have read her mind because now he was kissing her. Kissing her with an intensity all too terrifying and enticing at the same time. His lips molded to hers and she gloried in the gentle probing of his tongue.

Everything around her, including time, stopped. Her mind grasped for any shred of reality. She reached none. Nothing was real. Not the feel of his mouth, not the touch of his hand, not even the scent of his arousal.

His hand moved from her cheek into her hair. He wrapped the sandy tresses around his fingers, enjoying the softness. Before he knew what was happening his hand cupped her neck, pulling her closer. They needed to be closer. He'd never needed to be closer to anyone in his entire life. At first she hesitated, but his gentle prodding convinced her to let him into her own dream. He could feel her desire in the way her hands stroked against his bare flesh. The sweetness of her tongue against his was more than a little intoxicating. Her petal soft hands moved to rest on his chest and he sighed with relief. The smooth pads of her fingertips caressed tenderly, sending incredible waves of pleasure to all the right places.

Maggie stopped when he shifted underneath her. She wasn't sure what had possessed her to drag her nail around his nipple. Maybe she'd hurt him. When she opened her eyes and looked at his face, she knew she hadn't. His breath came in small gasps. His expression startled her at first, until he opened his eyes. His smoldering gaze stole her breath and she had to look away. Passion was too new to her, she had no idea where to go with it. What would he say when she told him she'd never willingly been with man? She'd heard enough talk to know some men loved the idea of being in control, but she needed that power. What would Paul do?

His hand moved away from her hair and slid down her back. All her fears subsided and she went down the path her desire led her. She sighed when he cupped her bottom and pulled her against him. Then she felt it. Pressed up against her lay the truth.

Maggie bolted up in her bed. She stared blindly around the room trying to remember where she was. "Oh thank God. It was just a dream," She choked out.

The soft patter of feet grounded her. She wiped her arm across her forehead and wasn't at all surprised to feel the perspiration.

"Maggie, are you okay?" Paul's voice came from the hallway.

"I'm fine. I had a weird dream. I'll be fine." *You'll*

be fine. Sure you will. Maggie lay back on the pillow and realized it was also wet, as was her T-shirt. Sweat. God, I'm covered in sweat. *You've got it bad, girl.*

Paul heard her settle back against the pillow. He remained standing outside her door until her breathing evened out. She wasn't asleep. He knew that. But she'd at least calmed down. This was the first time in a week she'd had a bad dream. Must be something in the air. He'd been on his way to the kitchen when he'd heard her tossing and turning. His own weird dream had startled him out of a sound sleep. He had no idea how long he'd lain in bed trying to catch his breath. Everything in his dream had felt so real. He could even smell her shampoo. His skin tingled with the recollection of her nails scraping against his bare flesh.

Something was going to have to give with Maggie. He needed his; but not if his dreams filled with her the sweet smell of her and the feel of her smooth skin under his hands. Tonight's dream had been the most vivid dream he could remember. He could still feel her silky hair wrapped around his fingers, the way she caressed his chest. Forgetting about his drink, he shuffled back to bed. There was very little of the night left and he needed to at least try to get some sleep.

The next few days proved interesting, to say the least, Paul made a point of avoiding Maggie. They brushed past one another in the kitchen in order to get coffee, but neither spoke unless absolutely necessary.

Maggie usually went and stayed in her room until she heard Paul drive away. She watched his car disappear down the road then gathered up her laptop and bag and headed for her own vehicle. She silently questioned what would be wrong today. Several times since she'd been in town she'd had to have some kind of repair done on the rental car. At first it had been more of a nuisance, but she was beginning to wonder if someone wasn't tampering with her car. She shivered when she remembered the orchids in her hotel room and her run-in with Packston Greely.

She climbed in and started the car. "All systems go." She'd carefully mapped out her plans for the day before leaving the house. First, she would meet Francesca at the library. The two had become friends, and Maggie wanted to help her with her current predicament. Francesca had no desire to marry Packston, and Maggie would do whatever she could to make sure she didn't have to. Maggie tried to remember what Francesca had told her about Packston's relationship with her father, but couldn't muster the thought. All she could think of were Paul's late night visits to the hall outside her room. It didn't really creep her out, but she couldn't help wondering why he didn't just ask to come in.

Maggie saw Holt going into Chaser's as she drove by. He turned and waved at her. A twinge of sadness seeped into Maggie's already foul mood at the thought of the closeness the brothers shared. Paul had spoken very highly of all his brothers and Maggie couldn't wash away the stains of jealousy. She couldn't remember how long it had been since she'd been a part of a family. Since she'd belonged. She blamed that on her job. She spent at least half of every month on the road, definitely not conducive to stability. But she'd made her choice and she couldn't regret it.

Maggie pulled into the library parking lot. Francesca sat waiting on the outside bench. She pulled her bag out of the car and ran toward the building. Francesca stood up and walked toward her.

"Hi, Maggie. I was afraid you weren't coming." Francesca wrung her hands.

"What's wrong? You look nervous."

Francesca glanced around before she spoke. "I found out something and I'm not sure what to do about it." She pulled Maggie by the hand toward her car. She unlocked the passenger side door and Maggie climbed in.

"Francesca, where are we going? Are you in some kind of trouble? I can help you, but you have to tell me what it is."

"I'm going to tell you, but not here. I want to go where no one will interrupt us. There are too many people here in town who know Packston and I don't think it's a good idea for them to see us together anymore."

Francesca climbed in behind the steering wheel and Maggie questioned silently whether Francesca was in any condition to drive. She managed fine as she pulled out onto the highway, heading toward the West

Bank. After driving off the ferry, Francesca expertly maneuvered the car through the streets of New Orleans. With the car parked in a small lot, the duo walked to the corner. Maggie stared ahead at the colorful murals painted across the building's walls. Francesca tugged Maggie into a doorway.

"What is this place?" Maggie asked as she glanced around the slightly crowded room. A spattering of shelves held a number of books. Scattered around the room were tables, hosting small groups. Several people also sat alone reading. No one noticed as they took their seats.

"It's Abstract's. I know we'll be safe here. Packston says it's the hangout for all the undesirable types."

It doesn't look like your normal coffee house."

"It's not. Most of these people live here, the rest are locals. They run the place in exchange for living space."

"Is it a half-way house of some sort?" Maggie turned several times, soaking in the myriad of colors covering the walls.

"I guess, maybe in a sense."

"That man over there is Judge Byron. When he isn't in court, he's here volunteering and helping keep things going."

"It has incredible charm."

"The people are nice and since they hold various addiction meetings to help those who want to get their lives straightened out, I know Packston won't follow me. I come here as often as I can get away." Francesca chose a table off aways from the others and they sat down.

"Francesca, tell me what you found out."

"I was at the Greely's last night and I heard Packston talking to someone on the phone. He was making arrangements for some kind of transfer."

Maggie took out her notepad and began taking notes.

"Maggie, he told the person on the other end of the line to make sure the exchange went off without a hitch. He said he didn't want anyone getting hurt."

"I have a feeling it's too late for that," Maggie said, glancing at Francesca.

"He said they couldn't afford any more attention than was necessary, until he'd taken care of his problem."

"That would be me." Maggie shook her head. *He has no idea.*

"I think you're right."

"Did he say what they were exchanging?" Maggie tried not to sound impatient.

"No, but it must be something big. He said the trucks would be at the site, and they could make the switch with no one being any the wiser."

"Francesca, think. Did he say where this would happen? I need to know exactly what you heard."

Francesca closed her eyes and Maggie could see her concentrating. Suddenly, her eyes popped open. "I do remember him saying that they could only do this next week. After that the opportunity would be gone.

He said, with all the commotion they would blend in."

Maggie tried to think of anything that could cause enough commotion to camouflage several trucks being loaded and unloaded. Of course, Mardi Gras. As much as she hated to admit it she was going to have to ask Paul for his help. She didn't know the area well enough to know about these things.

"Francesca, have you thought any more about breaking off your engagement with Packston? I mean things are getting pretty serious and I don't think you want to be in the middle of this."

"I spoke to my father and he pointed out that business was a man's job and I should just do what would be best for all of us. More or less he said I have to marry Packston."

Six

Francesca's words chafed at Maggie's mood. Another man who didn't know the value of a woman. How could any man send his only daughter into a den of lions?

"I think you need to just get it over with. Whatever these guys are doing is obviously illegal and dangerous. I worry about you. "Maggie saw the sheen of tears in her friend's eyes and reached for her hand.

"No one has ever really worried about me before. I'm glad you came to town. And, I'm glad you were persistent about talking to me. You're my only friend."

"I know exactly how that feels, Francesca. I've been alone so long, I was afraid I'd forgotten how to care about anyone."

Francesca smiled. "I don't see that it's been too much of a problem."

"It's easy caring about you."

Francesca patted her leg. "As easy as it is caring about Paul Remington?"

Maggie looked up, surprised. "What are you talking about? He's been very nice to me since I got here. If it weren't for him I'd be-"

"Cooped up in a small hotel room with no one to talk to?" Francesca laughed. "Yeah, I've heard that song from you already."

"I beg your pardon?"

"Don't. I know there is more to this than you're admitting to me, or yourself. Isn't it about time you came clean, with us both?"

Maggie pushed her oversized mug toward the center of the table. She looked over at her friend who didn't seem in any hurry to drop the subject.

"What makes you think I'd be the slightest bit interested in him? He's more arrogant than any man I've ever known."

"Arrogant, or right?"

"What do you mean?" Maggie asked.

"It seems to me you're mad because he saw you during a weak moment. Then he did a very noble thing by taking you into his home and offering you protection."

"I don't need his protection. I've been taking care of myself for a very long time."

"Maggie, what would you have done if he hadn't shown up in your room?"

"I would have-" Maggie lowered her head. "I don't have a clue."

"Okay, what about the nightmare? He sat in your room holding you all night and never made a pass. It seems to me like he's one of the few good men left in the world. Why fight it?"

"Fine, he's a noble kind of guy, but he still has a

bad attitude where women are concerned. He's not Prince Charming. He's just a nice guy."

"He's just a guy who puts color in your cheeks and makes your eyes sparkle."

"If you think he's so wonderful, you take him."

"I'm not the one who's falling in love with him."

"Look, Francesca. I don't have time in my life for love. I've worked hard to get where I am. My career is important to me, and I'm not giving that up for any man. No matter what he makes me feel like."

"Fine."

"Fine," Maggie repeated.

After a few minutes of companionable silence, the two women fell into a light conversation about their respective childhoods. One came from wealth, the other not. They discovered that despite their extremely different upbringing they weren't so different. Maggie sensed strength under Francesca's shy exterior. All she needed was the right man and some understanding and she would blossom.

"I think it's time we head back. I don't want anyone getting suspicious about you disappearing for so long." Maggie slid her chair away from the table. She hesitated before standing. "Thank you, Francesca."

"You're welcome. You can do something for me in exchange."

Panic rushed through Maggie and she feared for a brief moment that she might have made a mistake by trusting her new friend. "What?"

"Think about what I said, about Paul. Love is so

rare. If it falls into your lap, you should treasure it like the gift it is."

"I'll give it some thought," Maggie promised.

After paying their tab, the pair stepped back out onto the busy street. Maggie took in the sights around her as they wove through the crowds of tourists heading toward the parking lot. Several people bumped into them as they walked, mumbling their apologies. The New Orleans tourist district was still home to many. Maggie knew how they felt. Why did some people not understand the notion of personal space? Paul had made a point of always being just inside her space. No matter where she was he was never far behind.

With that thought fresh in her mind she shouldn't have been surprised to see him leaning nonchalantly against Francesca's car. He smiled when they stepped into the lot. She stumbled over a speed bump and nearly sprawled out at his feet.

"You okay, Maggie?" He reached out to offer his hand and she jerked away.

"I'm fine. What are you doing here?" she sputtered.

Maggie turned to find Francesca standing off to the side, smiling.

"I was just out driving and saw you two coming out of Abstract's. I thought maybe you'd planned a party and hadn't invited me."

"Something like that." Maggie stepped away from him and headed toward the far side of the car.

"Paul, would you mind giving Maggie a ride home. I have some errands to run and it would be a help if I didn't have to go all the way back to drop her off."

"You know me?" Paul looked at Maggie and she took her cue.

"Paul Remington this is Francesca Raynor. She's a friend of mine."

"You're Franklin Raynor's daughter, right? It's nice to meet you." He shook her hand and then turned his attention back to Maggie.

"Maggie mentioned that she'd been staying with you and since she doesn't know anyone else here. I figured you had to be Paul."

"So she's talked about me?" Paul winked.

Maggie stepped back toward him anxious to end his line of questioning. "Francesca, I could always go on your errands with you."

"No really. I'm sure Paul wouldn't mind your company one bit."

"It'd be my pleasure. And since it's not out of my way."

"Good. Then I'll be on my way." Francesca gave Maggie a quick hug and hopped in her car. Before Maggie could protest further, the car shot out of the parking lot.

"Why are you really here?" Maggie asked. She couldn't fight down the suspicion that he'd been following her. If she was right, she'd have his head on a stick.

"I saw you drive out of town and I got a little concerned. You know she's engaged to Packston Greely." He waited for her response.

"Yes. So?"

"Why would you even be seen with her? Have you lost your mind? If I can find you then Greely sure as hell can."

"Don't you dare talk to me like that. I'm not your wife," Maggie said and didn't know why.

"Dat's for damn sure, c*hère*. If you were my wife, you'd be at home where you belonged. I'd never be married to anyone who didn't have the sense to stay away from gangster's women."

Maggie listened, stunned, as a slight Cajun drawl slipped into his speech. It only seemed to show when he got angry.

"Well, I'm not your wife."

"*Non, chère*, not by any stretch of the imagination," he grunted back at her. "I don't want you around her anymore."

Maggie coughed and sputtered. She went so far as to clench her fist and seriously considered hitting him. A swift pop in the lip would do his attitude a world of good. She pulled her hand close against her side and clenched her teeth. "Oh, that's just great. Now, because you did me a favor, I'm not entitled to pick my own friends?"

"I din't say dat. You don't know what she's up to."

Maggie exploded. "She's up to being scared half out of her mind because her father is forcing her to marry a mobster who she doesn't like, much less love." She paused and took a breath. Paul started to speak and she cut him off. "I'm not finished. I came out here with her because she didn't want to put me at risk by being seen around town with her. She was trying to protect me, because we are friends."

"How do you know that?"

"Because she *is* my friend and I trust her. If she were out to get me would she have told me about the conversation she'd overheard between Packston and one of his goons?"

"What conversation?"

She had his undivided attention now. He didn't think she should be out looking for the information, but he wasn't too proud to listen to what she'd learned.

"They're arranging some kind of deal and they're making the exchange somewhere near here."

"What else?" he asked in a tone that made her feel like she was under interrogation.

Maggie stood with her lips pulled together. Something in his expression had changed. At first he'd been worried and irritated, now his face looked serious and anxious. He wasn't seeing her as a woman now. He finally saw her as a fellow reporter who had valuable information. She considered not telling him anything else, but something inside her urged her to take the good when she could get it. Maybe that was the ticket to getting to him. If she shared what she knew with him, maybe he'd see her in a different light.

"What else?" he urged.

"I'll tell you on the way home. But only if you buy me dinner."

His eyebrow shot up. But as he moved to open the car door for her, she hurried past him and climbed into the car by herself. She repeated what Francesca had told her during the drive.

During dinner, she carefully picked a few details she'd uncovered and shared them with him. Once they'd finished dinner he reluctantly agreed to take her to her car. They decided he would follow her home.

Maggie kept her eyes glued to the road. Over the last week she'd become fairly familiar with the winding roads, but huge holes in the roads, ignored by the city and state highway commissions, still made them dangerous. She made the turn off and headed down the last stretch of road toward the house. She passed only a few cars, the last of which caught her attention. A sleek, black, luxury car sped past her. She didn't remember seeing anything similar in Paul's neighborhood. As she came around a curve, the high beams of an oncoming truck temporarily blinded her. Just as the truck approached her, its lights went off.

"No, it can't be," she whispered. The truck slowed, suddenly veered toward her, and just before it hit her car pulled away from her. Maggie slammed her foot onto the brake pedal. She glanced in her mirror to make sure Paul was still behind her. The flash of his headlights reassured her.

When she stepped on the brake again, nothing happened. Her foot pressed all the way to the floor.

Panic flashed through her and ignited into terror. Her car flew around the curve and she couldn't stop it. The car continued forward. No matter which way she chose, she didn't see how she would get out alive. With that in mind she decided to jump and hope Paul didn't run over her.

She struggled with the seat belt, but couldn't get it to unlatch. With what little breath she had left, she heard herself scream. She grabbed the steering wheel with both hands and jerked it toward the guardrail. At least they'd be able to find her body.

Her heart hammered against her chest and the darkness closed in around her. The impact of the collision jarred her into oblivion. She kept her eyes open as the vehicle careened off the road. She had to do something. She tried to think. She tried to pray, but it wasn't God who came to mind. *Paul!*

"Maggie!" Paul gripped the steering wheel of his truck and kept his attention on the road in front of him. "What are you doing, Maggie?" He flashed his headlights hoping she would heed his warning. The car ahead of him swerved around the curve and threatened to cross the center line. He knew if Maggie lost control of the car she could plow through the guardrail and plunge nose first into one of the deep ditches.

The roads were wet with mist and she was moving way too fast. How did she think she could control thousands of pounds of metal at that speed? He resisted the clawing urge he had to stomp on his own accelerator. He kept the truck moving at a pace that wouldn't put him in too much danger, but one he could keep Maggie's Dodge in sight.

As quick as a flash of lightning, she was gone. The row of trees and bushes lining the road wound around and she was gone. "Calm down. She's right around the curve." His heart stopped and he wanted to close his eyes and will himself to her. Without warning a blinding pain shot through his chest and he feared he might pass out.

"Damn it, Maggie. What's wrong?" Paul tugged against the steering wheel and hoped it wouldn't come off in his hands. When he finally pulled around the curve, everything stopped. His foot came off the gas pedal and the truck slowed to a crawl. He stared numbly at the sight before him. It took several seconds for everything to register. When it finally hit him, instincts took over and he reacted.

"Oh, God." He slammed his foot on the brakes and his truck skid around to a halt. He jammed it into park and bolted out of the cab. Gravel crunched and his feet slid on the wet pavement as he ran toward the pile of mangled steel. He peered around the raised hood of the car. Plumes of smoke rose into the air and turned to steam. He moved to the car door. That's when he saw her.

Maggie lay hunched forward over the steering wheel. From his vantage point, he could see a trickle of blood as it ran down her cheek. His throat tightened and the air around him became too thick to breathe. He reached in through the broken glass and felt for a pulse. It throbbed against his fingertips, strong. "Thank God." Carefully he pulled his arm back out and went to work on the door.

He yanked and jerked on the handle, but it wouldn't budge. His hands ached as his sweating palms slipped against the metal.

"Maggie, you have to wake up." He didn't dare touch her again for fear of hurting her, but he kept talking to her. Maggie stirred briefly, but just as quickly, her head bobbed back down. He left her long enough to run back to the truck and call 911 on his cell phone. When he got back to the wreckage, she hadn't moved. Blood dripped into her eye and he used his shirtsleeve to wipe it away.

"Maggie, I need you to talk to me. I need you to tell me you're okay."

Maggie lifted her head and he saw the blood coming from a long gash at her hairline. She lifted her arm and let it rest against the car door. She cried out when she lifted her other arm. It fell back down against the seat.

Paul reached in and took her good hand in his while he waited for the fire department to come. Fortunately, he felt sure there was no danger of an explosion. He'd checked for leaking gas and sniffed for fumes.

"Maggie, why didn't you slow down? You know these roads are slick in the evening. Why were you going so fast?" Her hand trembled in his and he instantly regretted questioning her.

"I tried to-" she stammered. "I kept stomping on the pedal and the car kept going faster."

"You mean your brakes went out on you?"

"I wanted to stop, Paul. I swear I wanted to." Maggie gave a slight nod and he saw her hysteria beginning to rise.

"It's okay, Maggie. I know you did." Paul barely choked out the words before a tear slipped down his cheek.

"I wanted to stop. I wanted to make the car stop. It wouldn't."

"Hush, *chère*. Everyting gonna be fine. Dat ambulance is on its way and den we'll have you out of here in no time."

"Paul, I tried to jump and the buckle wouldn't release."

He reached around her and tried to pull the seatbelt apart. He could tell with his fingers that the release button was jammed. The wail of sirens tore Paul's attention from the buckle. He tried to pull away from Maggie. At first she wouldn't let him go.

"I'll be right here, *chère*. I need to get out of the way so they can get you out."

Paul stepped back when the bright red engine pulled up next to the wreck. Several men jumped out and pulled their tools from the side compartments. Maggie let her head fall back against the steering wheel and Paul watched as they went to work on the twisted metal. The sound of saws and glass falling to the pavement grated against his ears.

The captain pulled Paul off to the side and showered him with questions, all of which he answered with as much patience as he could afford. His eyes kept wandering back to the car. He watched to make sure they didn't hurt her when they pulled her out.

"Tell them to be careful. Her right arm is hurt and she has a huge cut on her forehead."

"They'll take care of her," the man answered sympathetically.

The ambulance arrived as the workers pulled Maggie out of the wreckage. They carefully placed her on a stretcher and the paramedics went to work. Paul watched as they took her blood pressure and checked for other cuts and breaks.

"Paul? Where's Paul?"

He heard Maggie's voice calling out for him and rushed to her side. Her face glowed pale and it nearly killed him to see the scrapes and blood on her face. He held her hand until the medics made him move back. He tucked the wool blanket up under her chin.

"I'll follow behind in the truck and I'll be at the clinic right behind you. I promise. Try not to be a pest if they ask you to do something." He tried to keep his tone light and teasing. Maggie rewarded him with a smile.

"I'll be good." She disappeared into the back of the truck and he watched as it drove off.

It wasn't until after he lost sight of the ambulance that Paul moved. He stopped long enough to bark off a few last instructions to the fire chief. "Make sure you have the wrecker take the car directly to the police impound in Algiers. Don't let them take it to Port Ray."

"It's your drive, Pal."

Paul climbed into his truck and hurried after the ambulance. He tried to concentrate on what could have happened to the brakes, but he could only focus on Maggie's pain. Her face had looked so pale and once again he'd seen terror in her eyes. The kind of terror he couldn't protect her from. "Oh, God." It was the same expression he'd seen on her face when she'd received the flowers and again when she'd had the nightmare. The kind of terror that could push a person over the edge. He wanted to keep her safe from the things that scared her. He wanted his brave and too proud Maggie back. He wanted her safe. If he'd have thought fast enough, he would have ridden with her.

Maggie didn't like weakness. Oddly enough in some instances it seemed to give her strength. She would be terrified. No. Not his Maggie. His Maggie? She'd be mad as hell if she thought he was taking care of her. She could do just fine without him. She'd told him that over and over. She didn't need anyone to take care of her. The trouble was, he needed someone to take care of.

Seven

God help him, he needed Maggie. He hadn't realized he could feel this way about someone after such a short time, but the truth of it, his feelings for her ran deep. Deep and straight into his heart. All he had to do was keep her out of trouble long enough to tell her so. That would change everything. Wouldn't it? She wouldn't be so quick to push him away once she knew how he felt; would she?

By the time he got to the clinic they'd already taken her inside. He squeezed his truck into a parking space and ran into the building. A man in blue doctor's scrubs met him in the hallway.

"Do I need to even ask if you're here about the girl they just brought in?"

"Don't start with me. Just tell me where she is, Eric."

"Not so fast, Paul. I need to take a look at her before you go pounding in there."

"I need Maggie to know I'm here. I promised her I'd be right here." Paul tried to shove past his younger brother, but didn't get far. He tried to move to the other side. Cut off again. "Stop it, Eric. I need to see her.

Now get out of my way."

Eric stood his ground. "Do you want me to throw you out of here, or are you going to behave?"

Paul stopped. He turned and faced the only sibling he'd ever been able to take in a wrestling match when they were growing up. He noticed for the first time that he'd somehow missed the changes. Eric stood only an inch or two shorter, but Paul wasn't so sure he could take him anymore.

"I'm assuming this is the Maggie, Holt told me about."

Paul snickered. "Good news sure travels fast in this town."

"From what Holt said I'm surprised she doesn't have you turning on a spit. He said you made a heck of a great first impression."

"Are you going to stand out here judging me and my big mouth, or are you going to go take care of Maggie so I can see her?"

Eric smiled and turned away. "I'll tell her you're out here, then when I'm done you can go in."

"Thanks."

Eric disappeared into the examining room and Paul collapsed into the closest chair.

Maggie flinched under the pressure of the doctor's examination. He checked her arms and legs and then took her to another room and took X-rays of everything. The first thing he'd said when he came in was that Paul was waiting to see her. Somehow, knowing that made things look a little brighter. The news she hadn't broken anything made it even better.

When she finally got a chance to look at the doctor, the recognition surprised her. It took her a minute to realize from where. Then she remembered the picture of Paul's family on the shelf. He had to be one of the Remington brothers.

"So how did you happen to get mixed up with the likes of my brother? He's not even the handsome one in our family," the man teased.

"Oh, I don't know. I do all right." Maggie felt loads better when she saw Paul standing in the doorway. He had dried blood on his face and his usually bright eyes were shadowed by dark circles. She noticed his forearms had bandages on them and she sat up.

"What happened to your arms? You didn't do that because of me did you?"

Paul swaggered into the room and leaned down next her bed. "Heck these are nothing compared to some of the scars your sharp tongue has left."

She knew he was teasing, but felt a twinge of guilt for the way she'd been treating him. So they didn't see eye to eye on everything. Big deal. "Do they hurt much?"

"Nothing a few therapy sessions with my shrink won't cure."

Maggie sighed. "I meant your arms."

"Oh those. I'll be fine. I have it on good authority that I'll heal. And so will you."

"So, I've been told. My shoulder is only twisted and should be better in a week or so."

Paul pulled up a chair and sat down. He glanced at his brother who promptly left the room. Paul took Maggie's hand and for a split second she hesitated, but finally relaxed.

"Maggie. I want us to go the cabin for a week or so. I have a place I share with a friend near Kenner. I think maybe we should let you heal without any outside stress."

"Paul, I don't know what this is all about, but I have a story to write and you hauling me off to Lord knows where isn't going to stop me."

"What's wrong with you, *chère*?" He stood up so fast it startled her. "You just about killed yourself; actually someone else just about killed you. You need some down time. I am not trying to stop you from writing this stupid story."

"Why do I find that hard to believe?"

"I don't give a damn what you believe. I was damn worried about you, and I don't think it's asking too much of you to go along with me on this."

Maggie watched his face turn colors as he bellowed at her. At first she'd thought he was angry, but his words said otherwise. She realized he'd been scared for her and he was trying to deal with his emotions.

"Never mind! You do whatever you want. I'm done with you. I don't have the time or the strength to argue about this. I hope you feel better."

Maggie's heart sank as he stalked toward the door. He reached for the door and took a step out. "Fine," she said softly.

"What?" He turned and looked at her.

"I'll go. But not because you bullied me."

"Then why?" His voice was no longer loud or angry. He let the door close, but he didn't go back near her.

"Because I think the time away will give me a chance to get the basis for my story written down. I can take my laptop and get all my new notes organized."

"Don't you ever quit?"

"Never. This is what I am. Take it or leave it."

Paul stared for a moment before he left the room. Maggie was afraid she'd pushed him too far. He'd left her. But she'd given him the opening. She'd let her damnable pride drive another man away. Why couldn't she just let somebody get close? She felt the tears welling up in her eyes and something squeezed her heart. The loneliness she thought was lessening, engulfed her. She turned her head when the door opened.

"Doc says you need to stay overnight. I'll go home and get our stuff and we'll leave here first thing." Without another word, he left the room.

Maggie's tears of loneliness turned into tears of joy, or something as close to joy as she was capable of. She drifted off to sleep with the image of him in her mind.

Her dreams came in erratic spurts. She woke several times with an eerie feeling of someone watching her, but each time she found herself alone. Images of the strange, but too familiar, truck raced in her mind. Then she saw her father. He tried to talk to her, but she couldn't hear him.

All at once the feeling changed. The short hairs at the base of her neck prickled and stood on end. She opened one eye and struggled to catch a reflection in the window. Finally, she rolled over.

"Ah, so you are awake. I was afraid I would have to find a way to wake you up myself."

"What the hell do you want?" Maggie reached for the nurse call button. A cold hand around hers stopped her.

"Oh, I don't think we'll be needing anyone else. I just came in to make sure you weren't hurt too seriously in your accident."

"How did you know about my accident?" Maggie scooted up toward the head of the bed and hoped she could look around him. Much to her dismay, he'd closed the door all the way. She couldn't see out and no one could see in.

"Maggie." He paused. "May I call you Maggie?"

"No. You don't need to call me anything." Her voice quivered and she felt weaker than she ever had in her life. "I want you to leave."

"And I want you to leave. I have enough trouble trying to fend off your nosy boyfriend. I don't need a second reporter snooping around making my life difficult."

"Look, I don't really care what you want or need. I came here to do a story and-"

He leaned down close to her.

"Get away from me." Maggie tried to push him away, but his fingers bit into her tender flesh and he held her in place.

"You should have listened the first time. If you had, this all could have been avoided."

Fear coursed anew and she felt herself slipping away. "You're the one."

"Take my advice and leave, while you still can," he said, his voice low and menacing.

She closed her eyes and tried to focus on what the man had said to her. When she opened them again, he'd gone. Rolling over onto her side, she curled herself into a ball and waited.

Paul drove home more by instinct than anything. His mind lingered on Maggie. He'd sensed that even in her vulnerable state she had her guard up. He'd been prepared to walk out the door and not look back. Thank God she'd stopped him. He couldn't imagine going to sleep and knowing she wouldn't be there in the morning, with her tousled hair and sleepy green eyes. He thought he might even be getting used to her stubborn modern woman's attitude.

Minutes later, he heard the phone ringing as he unlocked his front door. The machine kicked on before he could get to it, so he stood and listened.

"Paul, this is Francesca. I heard Packston say Maggie had been in an accident. I called to make sure she's all right."

Paul snatched the receiver off the hook. Everything fit into place all of a sudden. "Francesca. She had a small mishap, but she's fine. I'll tell her you called." He couldn't pinpoint why, but something about her didn't set well with him.

"Paul, listen to me. I think Packston and his brothers did something to the car. They were laughing and joking about making headlines. I thought you should know." She sounded sincere.

Paul paused. Could Maggie be right? Was Francesca on their side? "Thanks for calling, Francesca. I'll have Maggie call you when she's feeling up to it." He hung up the phone and ran up the stairs.

He found most of Maggie's clothes still folded in her bag. Obviously used to living out of a suitcase, he'd have to do something about that. He found stacks of papers piled on the desk and he scooped them all up and shoved them in her bag. After getting everything he thought she would need for their trip, which turned out to be most of her belongings, he went to his room and gathered his own stuff. Within an hour he was on his way back to the hospital.

When he stepped into the hospital room, he found Maggie lying on her side facing the window. Her hair had been washed and she appeared to be asleep. Paul crept into the room and stopped by her side. He watched the curve of her back shift with each breath she took. His fingers itched to reach out and touch her, to comfort her, but he held back. She needed her rest.

"What kept you?" She didn't look at him.

It didn't matter; he could see her face as clearly as if staring directly at it. "I had to get everything together and I had a phone call. Francesca sends her regards and wishes you a speedy recovery."

Paul stepped back as she turned over. She cradled her arm and tears welled up in her eyes from the pain of the movement. "How did she know what happened?"

"We'll talk about it after you sleep." Paul moved, but she reached out, grabbing frantically at his hand.

"Tell me, Remington." He rolled his eyes; she thought he would put her off again. "I need you to tell me what the hell is going on."

"She heard Packston talking to someone about taking care of you. She called to make sure you were all right."

"My God, Paul. They really want me dead. How can they be so dangerous?"

"I tried to tell you in the beginning, but you assured me you knew what you were dealing with."

"So now I get I-told-you-so?"

Paul leaned down as close to her as he could get without touching her. "You told me you knew all about it. I told you these guys were idiots, but dangerous. Packston is the ring leader and the other two will do his bidding with no questions asked."

"He was here."

"Who?" Paul asked, knowing who before she answered.

"Packston. He's the one who sent the flowers and probably engineered the accident. He confirmed it all."

Paul sat on the bed next to her and swept her into his arms. Maggie's voice shook with a weariness that matched his. "We just have to be very careful."

"I've done stories like this before and I've always been fine."

"Maggie, you should know this better than anyone, but nothing is ever what it seems to be. That's why there's a demand for reporters. To dig out the real answers."

Maggie saw the truth in his eyes. He'd warned her and she'd been too stubborn to listen. It had almost gotten her killed. "I'm sorry."

"Sorry won't save your neck when it's in a noose."

"I know. You just don't understand how hard it's been for me."

"*Chère,* it's hard for all of us."

Maggie pushed up and a sharp pain shot through her arm. "No. You're a man. It's different."

"No, Maggie. You've taught me something lately and I hate to admit it, especially to you, but we're the same. We're both looking for the perfect story to shoot us into stardom."

"But you have an advantage."

"*Non, chere,*" Paul argued. "I have to use the same words to write the stories. I have to use the same tools to get the truth. And I have to sell it to the same people as you. Where's my advantage?"

Maggie couldn't answer. Everything he said was true. Her gender could only be a problem if she let it. Maybe it was time she tried working with him, instead of against him.

"So, will I like this cabin you're taking me to?"

He smiled at her and the warmth of it began to melt the chill surrounding her heart. "If I have any say about it. Maybe, if you're a good girl, I'll show you the time of your life." His smile changed from warm to smoldering.

"I guess I'll just have to learn how to be very good then."

Paul settled back against the head of the hospital bed and Maggie settled against him. He sat still as she drifted into a fitful sleep.

Packston Greely stomped around his office. He yanked on the braided curtain cord and swore out loud. Word of Maggie Howell's accident had pleased him immensely, the rush of adrenaline almost as good as sex. The thought of sex brought his thoughts to Francesca. She'd been pretty scarce the last week or so, he figured the time had come to find out why. More than likely she'd been off somewhere with her nose buried in one of those ridiculous books she liked. He didn't have a clue as to why she needed to read trashy novels. If she was so all fired hot and looking for romance he'd give her a romp and show her what a real man could do for her.

News of Maggie's survival had not dampened his urge, it had simply made it more urgent. He had other ways of venting his frustration, but sex had always been his favorite. Maybe if he worked fast enough, he could trick Francesca into a night of stress relief.

He picked up the phone and dialed her number. After a half dozen rings his fiancé's voice filled the line.

"Hello."

"Francesca, I want to see you tonight." He didn't make requests. She was his woman and he had no intention of asking for permission to see her. He sat in the overstuffed leather chair and propped his feet up on the mahogany desk.

"Not tonight. I'm very tired."

He gripped the phone tighter in his hand, hating the way it trembled. "No. I haven't seen you all week."

"Packston, I sat at your house this afternoon for nearly three hours and you didn't have time to be bothered with me."

So, that's the way of it. She felt neglected. He'd wondered how long it would take her to feel that way. Most women needed constant attention, but he'd hoped her upbringing would have made her different. He didn't know too many twenty-six-year-old women who still lived at home with their fathers. He swung his feet back down onto the floor and exhaled. He was in no mood to argue. Why couldn't she see that?

"Well, I thought maybe we could spend some time alone. Just the two of us. I know I've been busy and I want to make it up to you."

Her silence irked him, but the she sighed. Packston assumed she'd finally realized how lucky she was to have him. Someone in the deal had to be lucky and it sure as hell wasn't him. She wasn't any big deal to look at and every time he tried to touch her she prudishly reminded him of her condition. At another time in his life he would have paid good money for a virgin, but not now.

He needed a woman who wanted to do it all the time. He had needs and he didn't have time to be bothered with begging. And why the hell should he beg for something he didn't even know would be worth a damn?

"I'm not asking, Francesca. I want to see you. Alvin will pick you up in thirty minutes. Be ready!" He slammed the phone down. Several pencils on his desk rolled onto the floor. The clutter of papers caught his eye and he questioned again why his father refused to allow him a secretary. He shouldn't have to take care of all this paperwork himself. What was the good of having money and power if you couldn't use it? Oh well, that would change soon enough.

He looked up to find his brother Alvin standing in the open doorway. "Pack, why you keep dat girly? She ain't no good."

"I keep her because I want to. My reasons are my own." *All five million of them.*

Alvin lowered his head and started to turn away. "Dat's your business. I'll be back with her soon."

"Did you want something or were you eavesdropping for no reason?"

Alvin stared down at his shoes. Packston thanked God he'd not been cursed with the same affliction as his two younger brothers. He had no tolerance for stupidity.

"I watched for dat reporter's car to come in, but it didn't."

Packston swirled his chair around and glared at his brother. The man took a step back.

"What do you mean it didn't? All accident cars go straight to police impound. Sylus is waiting for it."

"I'm telling you, I stayed right there and it didn't come in. Norbert's still watching."

Packston flew out of his chair and stalked toward his younger brother. "I want to know where that car is and I want to know an hour ago!"

Alvin turned to walk away, but stopped. Packston hated the vulnerability in his eyes and cursed his father for his lack of foresight in having more than one child.

"Should I get dat girly first?"

"Yes." Packston would have slapped the man had it not been for the shuffle he heard in the hallway. A second later, his father pushed around the corner, leaning heavily on his walker.

"Go, Alvin. I'll be in here when you get back." Packston stepped back and allowed his father into the room.

Packston stood impatiently until the old man settled on the leather couch. Finally, Packston sat down. The two men sat silently staring at one another until Anthony Greely finally spoke to his son. "I'm concerned."

Packston knew it was coming. It actually surprised him that it had taken his father so long to come to him. The old man was getting slow. "Why now?"

"I think you're in over your head. This is a bad time for the family and you're drawing unnecessary attention to us."

"Do you think I'm a fool?" Packston snorted. "Unlike your other offspring, I have a brain."

"You'll not speak of them in such a way." His deep voice bounced off the dark paneled walls. "They are no different from you and it would do you good to remember that."

Packston stood up and paced the room. If he planned on inheriting the Greely empire, he needed to bide his time. "I'm sorry, Father. I'm just frustrated today."

"Is it because of your failed attempt at disposing of the reporter?" The old man's eyebrow shot up. "I see I've hit a nerve."

"I didn't want to bother you with it. It didn't seem like it should be a problem."

"You assume I am also a fool. This is my business, my family. I know everything. *Everything*!"

Packston fought the urge to laugh out loud. He could think of several million things the old fool didn't know. "I only wanted to keep you out of this."

"Keep me out of my own business? Maggie

Howell has connections you would be well served not to underestimate."

"I'll handle her."

"What about Remington?" the old man asked pointedly.

Packston snapped the pencil he'd been holding in half. For as long as he could remember, the Remingtons had been giving him grief. His family would have even more power if not for their sanctimonious interference. "I'll handle him too. Now if you'll excuse me, I have to wine and dine my fiancé. She is feeling neglected."

"There are things we need to discuss." Tony Greely burst into a fit of coughing. His shoulders shook and Packston wondered how much more his father's tired old body could take.

"Later, Father. You need to rest." Packston pushed a button and a male nurse who resembled King Kong shuffled into the room. He lifted the old man into his arms and carried him off without a word. Packston made a mental note to die before he became a burden to his children. He was still standing at his office window when Francesca came in.

"Alvin said I'd find you in here." Francesca stepped into the room, but didn't go to him. He stood in front of the huge bay window staring out over the perfectly landscaped yard. She'd spent more than enough time out there to know there wasn't so much as an unevenly cut blade of grass. Packston accepted nothing less than perfection. She wondered why he'd picked her.

"I've had a trying day and I need you close to me." He reached out, but still didn't look at her. When she hesitated, he snapped his fingers. "Now!"

"If you're tired, I can go and we can do this another time." God, be merciful and let me go. He snapped again. Slowly she moved closer to him. When she stood within reach, he grabbed out and captured her arm.

She knew better than to struggle against him. It only served to infuriate him more. She stood stock still as he covered her mouth with his. His tongue scraped against her teeth until she finally wearied of the struggle and parted them. He grabbed a handful of her hair and jerked her head back. He mistook her gasp for passion and deepened the kiss.

Her stomach churned as she felt the bile rising toward her throat. It had been easier withstanding his pawing and groping before she knew what he was capable of. The thought of Maggie lying in a hospital bed tugged at her senses. She blocked out the feel of Packston's hands on her bottom and forced her mind to blackness. When he pulled away from her, she opened her eyes.

"You seem quite reserved tonight." His voice sounded patronizing and cold. She knew he'd expected her to fight him. But that wouldn't suit her plan. She had to gain his trust in order to be able to find proof of his involvement in Maggie's accident.

"Sit down." She led him to the sofa and coaxed him down. She placed her hands on his shoulders and began kneading the taut muscles. She cringed when he rolled his head back and leered at her.

Sheer determination kept her from jerking away and running. She'd get the proof Maggie and Paul needed, then she'd break off her engagement with Packston. To hell with what her father thought. Maggie had shown more concern and compassion for her in a week than her father had in a lifetime. Her father had let her down, but she wouldn't do the same to Maggie.

Thankfully, after nearly a half an hour the phone rang and Packston excused himself to handle some business. He said it might take a while. He strolled out of the room, but not before he forced himself on her again. No sooner was he out of sight did she spit into a garbage can.

She waited several minutes before running to the desk. She sifted through stacks of papers, not sure what she was looking for. She figured she'd know it when she saw it. By the time Packston came back she still hadn't found anything she thought could help. Thankfully, his business had distracted him to the point of silence. For the rest of the night they sat on the sofa while he stared off into space, which suited her fine.

Alvin dropped her off at home just before midnight. She called Paul's house, but got the machine.

Eight

Maggie laid awake watching Paul sleep. He'd pulled two chairs together and curled up in an awkward and painful looking position. His head bobbed sideways and he snapped it back into place without ever waking up. His sandy brown hair hung down over his closed eyelids making him look like a small boy. But he wasn't a small boy. He was a man. An extremely sensuous and passionate man. A man who had the ability to set her heart to thumping with a single look.

His lips pursed and a soft rumbling floated across the room. More than once she'd thought about kissing him, but he'd done nothing to indicate he wanted her to, until today. She'd seen the concern in his eyes and he'd made it no secret he cared for her. All she had to do was figure out what she wanted.

He shifted in his temporary bed and the lack of room and coordination sent him sprawling to the floor. He looked up at her when she laughed and buried her face in her pillow. When she looked up again, he stood over her. He looked exhausted and she knew it was her fault. She'd argued with him, trying to get him to go home to sleep, but he'd refused.

"You know, that bed is big enough for two."

Maggie stared at him. She'd been thinking the very same thing, but didn't have the nerve to voice her thoughts.

"Well, if I say no, I'll never get any sleep." She rolled over toward the edge, giving him the room he needed to climb in next to her. "At least I won't have to listen to you falling off the chairs all night."

Paul tried lying on his back. Then on his side. Finally, Maggie rolled over so her good shoulder was under her. "Put your arm over me."

"What?" he asked, looking more than a little surprised.

"We'll never get to sleep if you don't get comfortable."

Paul rolled onto his other side and carefully draped his arm over her. She nestled back against him and covered his hand with hers. The smell of his shampoo crept into her nostrils. She considered sending him back to his chairs, but refused to give up the feelings he sent spiraling through her. His breathing fell into sync with hers and she felt herself nodding off.

Maggie woke with a start. A sharp pain in her shoulder reminded her where she was. When she glanced at the window, she guessed it was just after sunrise. "Paul."

"Mmm." Paul nuzzled against her neck and his grip tightened around her waist.

Maggie instantly regretted waking him up. She felt safe in his arms, comfortable, like they were made to hold her.

"Paul. Wake up." Maggie squeezed his hand and shook him gently. Even the slightest movement hurt.

"You okay?"

Maggie could hardly think with his warm breath blowing along the back of her neck. Chills ran the length of her spine and goose bumps rose on her arms.

"I'm fine, just a little stiff."

"I guess we should see if the doc is around. We can get an early start and be at the cottage by breakfast."

Maggie smiled. A quick racing of her heart gave away her excitement about going away with him. She'd spent the better part of the night thinking about her stay in Port Ray.

"Did you tell your brother where we're going? I think they might worry if we disappear."

"They know how to get in touch with me if they need to, but under the circumstances the less they know the better."

Maggie nodded and let it go. She'd done enough arguing with him to last her a lifetime and she had other plans for this trip. If he wanted soft and domestic, she'd give it to him.

He slipped out of bed and ran his fingers through his mussed hair. His shirt pulled against his chest and Maggie watched, entranced, as the muscles in his forearms twitched. He pulled his arms over his head and stretched. Even lying down, the sight of his body made Maggie feel lightheaded.

Paul glanced at his reflection in the mirror and scowled. "God, I hate mornings."

Once she'd signed the release papers, Paul carried her to the car. She'd put up a token fight, but she secretly enjoyed the attention. She let her head settle on his shoulder. Must have borrowed some aftershave, she thought. She inhaled the woodsy scent and her insides twisted into a swirl of chaos.

The truck's engine cranked to life and they were off. She sat toward the center of the bench seat careful not to let her shoulder bump up against the door.

"Are you cool enough, Maggie?" When he looked at her and she felt more vulnerable than she cared for.

"I'm fine."

"Too cool? I have a blanket in back. I can pull over."

"Paul. I'm fine. Just drive."

"I brought all the papers from the desk in your room."

Her room. It sounded so right. She'd been comfortable at his house. He hadn't done anything extraordinary to make her feel that way. It was just natural. In fact most of her stay she'd been locked in her room refusing to let him do anything for her.

"Thank you. Did you find anything you didn't know?"

"I knew it was too good to last."

"Knew what?" Maggie asked, genuinely

perplexed.

"I threw everything in the bag. I didn't read it. Contrary to what you might think I am not the kind of person who can't keep his nose in his own business."

"I didn't mean to offend you. I just figured–"

"You just figured I would use your accident as a chance to use your own research to beat you to the finish."

"I wasn't aware this was a race." Maggie shifted in her seat. The truck slowed down and she caught Paul staring at her.

"I said I'm fine. We'll never get there if you slow down every time I move a hair."

"Forgive me for giving a damn," he snapped.

"Don't be rude."

"You know, I thought we were making some progress in this relationship, but I guess you're not willing to give an inch."

Maggie couldn't believe what she was hearing. A relationship? Was that what he wanted? Was she even capable of a relationship with him? Past experience said no. But Paul was different. He had qualities she admired. The reality of it struck her as ironic. Ever since her parent's death, she'd wanted to be the very best at what she did. Now, looking at him, she didn't have a clue as to what she wanted to do.

"If I agree to give an inch will you give me another chance?"

"Possibly."

Neither one spoke until they reached the cottage.

Maggie sat inside the truck staring at the cabin. The single story structure looked quaint and cozy. She'd never thought of herself as an outdoorsy type person, but she could easily be persuaded to live out the rest of her life here.

A circle of spruce trees stood guard around the cabin, protecting it from all the evils of civilization. A sparse spattering of color enhanced the peaceful setting and she found comfort in the wildflowers.

She let Paul carry her inside and she didn't argue when he gave her instructions on what she could and couldn't do.

"You will lie on the couch and do nothing. If you need something, you call me and I'll get it for you." He stood in front of her with his arms folded across his chest. "Got it?"

"Yes, sir!" She waited until he'd walked to the front door, before she stopped him. "Paul? There seems to be a flaw in your tyrant theory."

"What's that?"

"I don't think it's going to make me feel any better if you go to the bathroom for me." She forced a cough and covered her mouth to hide her smile.

"Very funny, Howell. Just rest!"

She watched with interest as he carried several loads of wood in from outside and started a fire. Despite the heat outside, there was a slight chill in the cottage. She figured it to be the dampness from the swamp. Her breath caught in her throat when he bent over to stoke the flames.

Staring back at her from across the room was the most incredible rear end she'd ever seen. A butt to die for. "Oh Lord."

He turned around and caught her staring. "See something you like?"

"I–uh–er–" The broad expanse of his shoulders filled the room. His chest tapered down into a slender waist that further fed the picture of near perfect physical condition. Maggie's eyes traveled the path from neck to navel. It was when her wandering eyes reached the lower regions she realized he was watching her.

"Does it meet with your approval?"

She felt her cheeks change colors at least a half a dozen times. She knew because, with each shade her cheeks blushed, the fiery feeling in them intensified. "I'm sorry, I didn't mean to stare."

"I'm sorry to hear that. I was kinda hoping that was a spark of interest flashing in your eyes."

"You flatter yourself, Remington," Maggie said, half teasing. She considered fessing up, but his arrogance and self-assuredness set her defenses on red alert. Whether it was interest or not, what right did he have to call her on it?

She looked up in time to see him smile at her and head toward the cabin's small kitchen. She listened while he clanged pots and pans around on the counter tops. From the sound of things he was making a horrible mess. Thank goodness she wouldn't be expected to clean up after him.

"Breakfast will be ready in five minutes. I just want to clean up a little."

Maggie smiled. Mr. Macho had a domestic streak that would make Martha Stewart proud.

He appeared in front of her carrying a plate heaped with eggs, bacon, and a decadent looking cinnamon roll. He set a tray across her lap and tucked a napkin under her chin.

"Thanks, Dad." She hadn't meant to be sarcastic, but his scowl said he'd caught her sharp tone. "I was just kidding."

"I don't do this for just anyone." The wrinkle across his brow lessened, but didn't go away completely. He sat next to her on the sofa and silently ate his own breakfast. He stared straight ahead.

She watched him, hypnotized with the way the muscles in his neck worked as he chewed, then swallowed. Guilt swelled inside Maggie. Until this very second, she'd never even considered whether or not he'd been involved in a relationship before she came along. Something inside her ached to know he hadn't been. When she looked at him again she thought it was a long shot. His dynamic good looks and the fact that a good chunk of the female population would kill for a man who wanted them barefoot and pregnant, not to mention pampered and coddled. What did they know that she didn't?

"There's more if you're still hungry." He reached out for the plate and she plucked the rest of her roll off it before she gave it to him.

"No, this is fine." She savored each bit of the sticky, sweet glazed bun while he was gone. She maneuvered herself off the couch without causing herself too much discomfort. She turned around to find him watching her, but he didn't move until she steadied herself. Then he moved close. Very close.

He leaned toward her and she felt his breath on her chin. Without any further warning his mouth was on her. Not on her mouth, but on her chin. His tongue danced a trail up until it tickled the corner of her mouth. Her heart pounded and her eyes instinctively closed. Lightly, he sucked on her lower lip. When his tongue skidded across the same lip she fell. She knew she was physically standing, but she had fallen into some swirl of emotion quickly stealing her common sense away. She didn't know how she felt about the man doing these incredible things to her. She also didn't know why she didn't want him to stop.

He stopped. Instantly, her entire body began to ache, he kept his hands on her, but he'd stopped his torture. They stood as close to her as two people could be without being one. No part of him touched her, but his aura, the sense of him wrapped around her and warmed her from the inside out.

"Paul." She hadn't meant to speak and she hadn't meant to make him move away.

"I'm sorry." The words tumbled out of his mouth as he backed away. "I didn't mean to do that. You had icing on your chin."

Her fingers moved up to her lips. She brushed at

the moisture from his tongue. The same tongue that only seconds before had been doing wonderful things to her. "Paul, do you have a girlfriend?" Subtle, Maggie. Very subtle.

"Not for a while. I don't have very good luck with women." His answer came as somewhat of a surprise. "I tend to be overbearing."

"Really?" The word dragged out with a hint of teasing.

Her eyes sparkled and he saw her relax. He needed her to stop looking so delicious or his breathing would never return to normal. He clenched and unclenched his fists. *Relax!*

She'd pulled her hair back in a clip and he couldn't stop staring at her totally exposed neck. A neck so slender and tempting he couldn't see straight. The neck of her over-sized T-shirt slid down off her shoulder and the bare flesh called out for him to touch it. His fingers itched to feel its ivory softness.

"I can't believe that. I'd kill to have a man like you."

Paul held back his chuckle as she sputtered to explain her words.

"I mean you can cook and everything. Heck, you even like to cook."

"It's all right, Maggie. I know what you meant." He lifted his hand to pull her shirt back up. He couldn't bear to look at her bare flesh anymore. His fingers brushed against its softness. They lingered long enough to send him into a downward spiral of desire.

"I think–"

"I can't think." She leaned her head back and gazed into his eyes. He advanced on her again, but she held her ground. So proud and defiant. She had to know he was going to kiss her. He could see the traces of fear in her eyes, but she didn't back down.

"Do you feel it?"

She held his gaze as he moved against her. "Feel what?" There was nothing coy in her question. It was self-preservation he heard. If she fought him, it would be the same as admitting she did feel it.

Paul's anger flared at her denial and he felt his control slipping. Careful of her sore shoulder, he wrapped his arm around her waist and drew her all the way against him. Their bodies fit together so perfectly they might have been made as one then separated. "Feel this," he whispered as his lips took hers.

He kissed her, so completely the urgency of it scared him. Her mouth, soft and wet, held him at bay, at first. Then, as his hand caressed her back, she relaxed and folded into his arms. When her lips parted, he lost what little self-control he'd clung to.

Maggie wrapped her good arm around his back and pulled him against her. Her mind screamed, *Stop*, but her lips begged for more. His lips were more persuasive than she cared to admit and she was helpless to pull away. One arm held her tight, while his other reached up to pull her hair loose from its clip.

His fingers tenderly massaged her scalp as he loosened the hair. His mouth lifted slightly from hers.

"Tell me to stop, Maggie." His voice cracked with huskiness and emotion.

She should. There was no doubt in her mind they should stop. Okay, maybe a small doubt. After all, what was wrong with enjoying something so innocent? Her inner struggle continued and he must have got tired of waiting for her to stop him, because he went back to kissing her again, this time soft and excruciatingly slow. Holding her against him, he backed them up against the sofa. Turning his body to absorb the fall he gently lowered them down onto the cushions. Maggie turned so her shoulder was away from him and positioned herself across his lap. Her hand went instinctively to his shoulder and pulled him against her.

Where did she find the strength or courage to be so bold with him? She'd never come close to being in this situation with a man before. Except him. She had no idea what she should do. Even if she knew would he want her to?

She gasped for air when his lips moved down to her neck. She trembled as his tongue flicked against her ear lobe. He nuzzled against her and she sank into his warmth, savoring his tenderness. Giving in to the feeling, she relaxed against him. His sigh of longing was drowned out by the pounding on the front door.

He looked into her eyes and she knew whatever had just happened was far from finished. It would be, maybe not now, but it would be finished. He lifted her off his lap then thundered toward the cabin door.

While Paul dealt with their visitor, Maggie kept herself busy by setting up her laptop. She searched for a phone, and found none. She did however find a phone jack in the kitchen. Just to make sure, she hooked her modem up and was thrilled to find it worked. She heard Paul moving around the main room as she wrote an email to Joe. It had been days since she'd been in contact, and she knew he'd be worried. When she collected her own mail, she found several frantic notes from him. He'd been contacted about her accident and his notes all but pleaded with her to come home.

She explained in her note that she had things she had to follow through on before she could even think about coming home. She didn't, however, tell Joe that none of them had anything to do with her story.

"I see you found everything all right."

Maggie looked up at him. "Everything is fine. I needed to check in with Joe. Who was at the door?"

Paul rustled around the kitchen putting things away and basically avoiding eye contact with her. "The caretaker came to tell me my friend will be up here on Friday, so we have five days."

Maggie figured it was more than enough time for them to sort everything out. He left the room and came back with his own computer. He set it directly across from hers and ran an extension to a separate plug. For the better part of the day they exchanged information and typed notes into their respective files. Somewhere during the day they agreed to work together for the rest of the story.

"I know you wanted to do this on your own, Maggie, but I don't think it's a good idea."

She stopped typing and stared at him. "I'm assuming this has nothing to do with your need to keep me safe," she remarked sarcastically.

"Not entirely. I think if we work together we can get a lot more ground covered and maybe even get done quicker. You're supposed to have your story in by the end of the week and I'm due now."

"I think I have more than enough to actually finish the story, but I'd like to know more about this supposed exchange."

Paul shuffled through a stack of papers and slid one toward her. Maggie picked it up and read it. "You mean Greely trucking is the company delivering the supplies to the St. Charles Street businesses?"

"From what I can tell Anthony Greely tried several times to become a member of the *Mystic Krewe of Comus*, without success. In New Orleans being a figurehead in the carnival is a sign of acceptance and status. When that didn't happen, he did the next best thing."

Maggie understood. "He made it so everyone who had shunned him, would need him to get the things they need to get through Mardi Gras."

Maggie flipped through several pages of notes. "How did we miss all this before?"

"It was news to me too, but it seems your friend, Francesca, really gave us something to look into."

"You don't trust Francesca, do you?" Maggie waited for his reply. He was obviously considering his answer very carefully.

"I didn't, but when she called last night she sounded genuinely concerned. I think she's on the level. I just don't understand why she's with grease boy in the first place."

"I think it's more her father than anything. She doesn't like Packston, much less love him."

"How can you be with someone you don't love?" He looked directly at her and she was thankful for the distance between them. Although it did little to protect her from the heat of his stare.

She'd almost given in to him. If the caretaker hadn't come to the door, she would have, but she didn't love him–did she?

Nine

Unsure of why his mention of love had sent her heart into overdrive Maggie shrugged and immersed herself in her work. Neither one of them said anything else about it. They spent the next several days pretending ignoring the sparks and sexual tension snapping in the air around them, or trying.

By Thursday night, Maggie was so exhausted from dodging his playful questions and insinuations she could have spit. Twice during the week, they'd been caught up in a moment, but the moments hadn't lasted. Paul had slept on the sofa from the beginning and Maggie had spent most of the night listening to him toss and turn. Not that she could sleep anyway. He'd gotten her to agree to a night out and she found herself looking forward to it.

The next morning, Paul informed her he was on strike. He'd burned his hand cooking breakfast and he didn't want to cook anymore.

"If you're hungry, you'll have to fend for yourself."

She understood his foul mood. She'd caught herself yelling at the crickets keeping her awake just before dawn.

"Tell you what, Grumpy. I'll fix dinner tonight."

"Why?"

His question caught her off guard. "What do you mean, why?"

"Just what I said. Why are you going to cook dinner?"

"Because, you've been very nice taking care of me and waiting on me hand and foot and I'd like to do something nice for you." She tested her shoulder raising it and stretching her arm out to the side and then down. "Besides, I think I'm almost back to normal and I want to prove that–" She stopped unable to finish telling him she wanted to prove she could be just as domestic as the next girl.

"Fine." He left the room without another word.

Maggie looked around the kitchen. Not her domain, but she could pull it off. She only knew how to cook one thing and she didn't know if she even had any of the ingredients she needed. They'd stopped and picked up some groceries on the way. She decided she'd just have to make do.

Upon further investigation she found everything she needed to make beef stroganoff except the noodles. She did find a cookbook and all the ingredients to make them from scratch. The closest she'd ever come to making anything from scratch was hot cocoa from a pouch. How hard could it be? She pulled everything together and went to work. She knew the noodles would need all day to dry so she could cook them. So she started with them.

She wasted a half a dozen eggs trying to separate the yolks and the whites. She wore only one shoe. The other was soaking in the sink so the yolk wouldn't stain the white canvas material. The hardest part of her noodle adventure proved to be the rolling of the dough. It took a while to get the hang of the flour and finally the mixture stopped sticking to the rolling pin.

"Blast it all to–" She cussed when a hole appeared in the center of the slab.

Paul stood in the doorway watching her. She was covered from head to toe with flour and the kitchen didn't have a prayer of surviving. She hobbled across the room with one bare foot to get more flour. He wondered where her other shoe was. He thought if she needed more flour she could shake some from her hair. Although, the powder frosting her brown tresses didn't look as out of place as the smack of egg yolk on her cheek. Thankful she hadn't noticed him watching her, he continued to follow her every movement with his gaze.

She hummed softly as she cut the dough into thin slices and laid them out to dry. Once she'd finished, she stopped and looked around the kitchen. "Oh my, did I do this?"

Stepping out of sight before she caught him, Paul decided that if she could pull off this meal he would clean the kitchen for her. Maybe it was guilt for yelling at her. Maybe he just wanted to do it. What did the reason matter, and who did he have to explain himself to?

Paul walked outside and sat on the porch. With his feet up on the rail he went over the last few weeks in his mind, from the first moment he'd learned Maggie was coming, to now. She'd gone from defiant Ms. Independence to June Cleaver. The change wasn't altogether bad. In fact he liked watching her in the kitchen, but he also longed to see more of her spirit and spunk. The truth of it, he liked their verbal sparring matches. He liked the way her hazel eyes sparkled gold when something got her dander up. He liked the sexy way she pouted when she fell behind in the game and he had the edge on her. He liked the way she watched him through lowered lids when she thought he wasn't watching.

A little while later, Maggie called him in for dinner. He walked in to find the table set and candles lit. She had changed clothes, but the flour clumped in her hair told him she'd not showered.

"Everything looks wonderful. Is there anything you need me to do?"

"You can open the wine. There was some in the pantry so I chilled the red." She handed him the bottle and he went to work on the cork.

He filled the glasses while she set the food out. Everything looked perfect. A fragrant steam rose above the bowl holding the stroganoff and another bowl held her homemade noodles. Paul smiled. He had to give her credit. She'd worked a miracle.

"Hand me your plate." She took the stoneware

dish and put a thin layer of gravy in the center. He watched expectantly as she dished noodles onto the plate. She leaned a little as she filled the plate. He assumed her shoulder was still weak. It wasn't until she handed him his plate that realized the truth. Expecting it to be light, the added weight in his hand caught him off guard. He quickly recovered as the plate banged on the table. He guessed it to be at least twenty pounds of food.

She filled her own plate and sat down. Out of respect, Paul toasted her culinary skill and they drank. His first bite was beef. The flavor was outstanding and he sensed there might be hope. When he lifted the fork full of homemade noodles into his mouth, the bottom dropped. He chewed. He didn't know what else to do. He struggled to scrape the doughy substance off the roof of his mouth without her noticing.

"This is the best beef stroganoff I've ever had." *Good thing it's the only stroganoff I've ever had*, he thought, thankful he didn't have to lie. Her face lit up, he wanted it to stay that way. She looked beautiful. The candle light cast shadows that enhanced her regal features and he felt something hit in the pit of his stomach. He figured it might have been the noodles, but knew it was more than likely his heart.

While they finished eating they chatted about different stories they'd done. Paul realized she really did have all the experience of which she'd boasted. He'd read some of her stories and they were good. Better than good. They were top-of-the-line. When they were done, they cleared the table together. Just before they pushed through the kitchen door, she stopped him.

"Paul. I'm really sorry about the kitchen."

He looked at her and knew he didn't want to go in there, but he couldn't escape the inevitable.

He pushed in and couldn't believe his eyes. The counters were white. No signs of the polished oak. The stove had morphed into a mass of congealed starch and the floor was beyond hope.

"It shouldn't take me long to get it cleaned up," she told him meekly.

He hated it when she got soft. So he did the only thing he could think of to make her stop. "Maggie you'll be old and gray before you get this place cleaned up." That did it.

Her eyes flashed while her cheeks flamed. "I doubt that. Just don't you worry about it," she snapped.

"Well, let's get started Mrs. Crocker." She spun around away from him, but he caught the flash of her smile.

It took them over an hour of side by side cleaning to get the kitchen back in order, but the end result was worth it. The appliances sparkled and the wood counters glowed. As they walked out of the kitchen Maggie stopped and turned around. Unprepared for her movement, Paul plowed into her. His hands reached out instinctively and grabbed her. He wondered why it felt so natural to reach out and hold her.

"I forgot to turn off the oven." She looked up at

him and his heart melted.

"I got it a few minutes ago." Their gazes locked and Paul's knees went weak. "Maybe I'll double check; it really is hot in here."

"Yeah."

When he came back out, she lay curled up on the sofa staring into the fire. Without saying anything he leaned her forward and slipped in behind her. Together they stared into the fire until the last bit of wood glowed red. The room had begun to chill, a storm brewed outside blowing cool air through open windows, but neither one of them got up. Maggie reached up and pulled an afghan off the back of the couch to cover them. She leaned against him and he wrapped his arms around her. Paul didn't know who moved first, but suddenly they were kissing. There was enough fire between them to melt Alaska.

She responded to his kisses with kisses of her own. Her hands roved over his chest and her fingers laced up around his neck. Without moving away from her, he lifted her off the couch and carried her into the bedroom.

He lay next to her and his hand set out to exploring. He ran his fingertip down from the hollow of her neck until it found the top button of her blouse. He hesitated, giving her the chance to stop him. She didn't.

He flicked the row of buttons opened to find her barely covered by a thin wisp of lace bra. The pad of his thumb brushed against the lace and she shivered.

The sigh that accompanied the shudder told him she was anything but cold. The tightness in his jeans grew uncomfortable and he needed to find some kind of relief. He took her hand and pressed it down to the button of his pants. Her fingertips brushed against him and he almost cried out.

"Oh." It was Maggie who cried out.

He closed his eyes when he realized the pounding he heard wasn't his heart. He lay still listening to the sounds of someone moving around in the front room of the cabin. When he opened them he glanced at the bedside table. The red numbers on the clock radio flicked over. Midnight. The start of a new day. The start of–"

Then reality hit him. Someone was in their cabin in the middle of the night. He covered her mouth and told her to stay completely quiet. The fear he saw in her eyes was almost more than he could stand. He wanted to wrap his arms around her and make that fear go away. He'd almost given in when–*Slam!*

"Stay here." Paul crawled out of the bed and grabbed a baseball bat leaning in a corner of the room. "It might just be kids out looking for trouble."

Maggie grabbed at her clothes and scurried out of the bed after him. "Or it could be Packston or someone who wants to kill us."

Paul stopped and looked at her. "Then that's even more reason for you to stay right here."

"What's to say you can swing that thing any better than me?" Not that she wanted to, but she couldn't help the resentment she felt at him assuming she couldn't take care of herself.

His face grew red from anger and he thrust the bat toward her. "Fine, Maggie, you go out there and defend us. You're absolutely right, there isn't one damn good reason why I should go out there and try to protect someone who fights me at every turn."

"Wh–wh–"

"No, really, I want you to do this. It was insensitive of me not to consider the fact that you might want to get your head knocked off by some doped up kid looking for trouble." He bowed in grand gesture and stepped back away from the door.

Several loud bumps and a curse brought them back to the present problem. Maggie's eyes grew wide.

"Give me the damn bat, Maggie and don't you come out of this room or I'll use it on you." In a flash, he was gone. He ran into the room screaming like an idiot; that alone would have scared off the devil himself. The equivalent of an eternity passed before she couldn't stand it anymore. Maggie tiptoed to the door and eased it open enough to see out. She couldn't see anyone, so she opened the door further. None of the furniture had been disturbed and she saw no signs of a struggle. She crept toward the kitchen, her heart pounding in her chest. What if someone had knocked Paul unconscious? What if whoever it was knocked her out? For a split second she thought about slipping out the front door and running for help, but a noise in the kitchen caught her attention. Was someone laughing?

"How long you gonna leave her in there?"

Maggie didn't recognize the voice, but she knew she was the subject of conversation. She stepped up to the door and slammed her hand against it. "Yes, Paul, how long *are* you going to leave me in there?" She stomped into the kitchen and faced the two men sitting at the wood table. Paul tipped his cup of coffee in her direction and smiled. "Well, I don't have to figure that out since you decided to ignore me–again."

The stranger handed Paul a twenty-dollar bill and burst into a fit of laughter. "You win."

Maggie's nostrils flared as she stared the two laughing men. "Jerk!"

Paul's voice followed her out of the room. "I'm pretty sure she meant me."

Paul cringed at the sound of the bedroom door slamming. He finished his coffee and left the kitchen. He didn't say anything when he entered the bedroom. He simply stood and watched Maggie stuff her clothes into her bag. Suddenly, she stopped and her shoulders began to shake. Paul took a step toward her, but stopped when her head snapped up.

She didn't look at him. "Are you taking me back, or do I need to rent a horse?"

Paul wanted to apologize for teasing her, but she didn't give him a chance. She flung the bag over her shoulder and pushed past him. "Maggie, you should have let me introduce you to–"

"I'll be in the truck."

Another door slammed and Paul stood alone in the

bedroom. Her scent lingered and every muscle in his body tightened at the thought of her body pressed against his. He'd probably never know what would have happened if they hadn't been interrupted.

The trip back to Port Ray had to be among the longest he'd ever made. At least a dozen times he tried to apologize, only to be silenced with a glare cold enough to frost a snowman's butt. Maggie didn't appear to be in any mood to forgive. Paul thought she really should try to get a sense of humor. Then again, her lack of humor had won him thirty bucks, twenty for her not waiting for him and five for each of the two slamming doors. He could make a killing off her. He grinned and she harumphed him.

"What is so funny?"

"Nothing, I was thinking about something."

Maggie turned back to the window. "I can only imagine."

When they finally pulled into the garage, Paul hesitated before getting out of the truck. "Maggie, I think we need to talk."

Maggie climbed out of the truck cab and slammed the door. She ignored the bag in the bed and let herself in the house. She turned to him before closing the door. "Perhaps you should think again." She climbed the stairs and locked herself in her room, where she stayed for the better part of two days.

Ten

Since their interrupted session at the cabin, things had been strained, to say the least. Maggie had almost given in to Paul and that could have been disastrous. Thank goodness his friend had shown up when he did. They'd been back at his house for two days and he'd been sickeningly sweet to her. She'd finally told him to leave her alone. That had put things back to normal. He'd been barking at her ever since. She hadn't slept a wink since. Maggie stared at herself in the mirror. She frowned at the dark circles under her eyes.

"Come on, Maggie, we're going to a Mardi Gras festival for cripes sake. You don't have to do all that woman stuff."

Maggie stood leaning against the bathroom counter. She looked at her watch and decided to make him wait five more minutes. She'd had just about enough of his smart remarks about women and their habits. A little waiting would do him good.

"I'll be right out," she lied.

"You said that five minutes ago."

Since she'd gone into the bathroom, Maggie had rearranged her makeup bag, refolded her towels under the sink, and cleaned her toothbrush. Her things, it amazed her how naturally her things fit into his life. She had been tempted to put her makeup in the drawer, but a small doubt held her back. It would only be a matter of time before they would finish the story and then Paul would send her back to Shreveport.

She glanced at her watch and decided it was time. Let's see if he can pass this test, she thought. She had put on minimal makeup, and pulled her hair back in a basic ponytail. Would he notice the wasted time or would he lie about how dazzling she looked? She opened the door and stepped out into the hallway.

Paul stared at her and opened his mouth to speak. He shook his head and snapped his mouth shut. "Let's go, before we miss all the excitement."

Maggie smiled. At least he hadn't lied. "You know we don't have to do this. You don't seem like you're in any mood to have fun."

"Oh no, I don't want you to have any reason to say I cheated you out of a big story. Besides, I think a night out without work will do you–us both some good."

"I happen to like working."

Paul stared at her. "So do I, but a night out never killed anyone. Besides, in a way we will be working."

Paul grabbed her hand and dragged her down the stairs. Maggie waited for him to let go of her hand. When he didn't, she smiled. When they got to the truck Maggie reached to open her door and Paul smacked her hand.

"Stop it, Maggie. I'll get it."

"I can get it myself," Maggie argued.

Paul sighed. "Okay, let's establish something right now. I am perfectly aware that you can do anything I can do, but better. You've pointed that out repeatedly. But I don't give a flying flip. You agreed to go out on a date with me on my terms and these are my terms."

"You can't be serious."

"Pay attention, *chère*. You will not open one single door tonight if I am within ten feet of you."

"Paul–"

"Shh. You will not shell out one single penny for anything."

"That's not fair. What if I want something?"

"Then you bat those beautiful lashes of yours and find a way to manipulate me into getting it for you."

Paul folded his arms across his chest and Maggie had an overwhelming urge to smack the smug smile off his face. At the same time she hoped he hadn't noticed her blush at his backhanded compliment.

"You *are* serious."

"Take it or leave it."

Maggie remembered her ultimatum in the hospital. She'd set the ground rules for her return to his house. She figured he'd earned this. After he opened the door, she brushed past him and climbed into the truck. She folded her hands in her lap and Paul slammed the door shut with a satisfied smile.

The drive took nearly an hour, but Maggie enjoyed the scenery. The closer they got to the city, the larger the groups became. Masses of people loitered everywhere as Paul maneuvered the truck through the crowded streets of the city. Many had been blocked off, making it nearly impossible to find a spot to park. Maggie listened to Paul chatter on about some ideas his brother had to redecorate Chaser's. She liked Holt and hadn't spent much time at his bar. But the brothers went out of their way to make her feel like she belonged in Port Ray, but doubts still shadowed her.

The blue of the sky melted into a spray of flashing oranges and pinks reaching toward forever. Maggie lost herself in the changing colors, watching the hues blend into a canvas of brilliance. The blazing ball of fire slowly slipped down behind the wrought iron encased buildings.

Paul steered the truck around a sharp curve and then Maggie saw it. The brightest shades of red, orange, blue, purple and every other color imaginable stretched farther than she could see. Ornately decorated headgear bobbed along the streets. Drunks staggered along the blocks, bumping into fellow partiers. Maggie looked over to find Paul's blue eyes sparkling with the intensity of the city's bright lights. The big strong man next to her had miraculously transformed into an anxious child.

"You like carnival?" Maggie could see the answer in the way he fidgeted in his seat.

"My mother brought us every year, no matter what. One year we came in a rainstorm. That was the year I saw a two-headed cow walking along the street.

I had nightmares for months."

"You must have quite an imagination to enjoy this so much."

"It's all part of the history. There's no place more alive than New Orleans during Mardi Gras." Maggie reached for the door handle, but stopped when she glimpsed his expression. She waited in the cab of the truck, patiently, while Paul dawdled around. He checked all the switches in the truck. He checked the bed cover and actually had the nerve to pull out a towel and wipe some imaginary smudge off his fender.

Maggie sat and waited. He could toy with her, but she could take it. Without a word, she acknowledged his dare for her to open the door herself. Not a chance. If he wanted to play this game, she'd just have to readjust the rules to suit her. When Paul finally opened her door, she remained seated. She turned her head slightly and smiled at him. She swiveled to the side and reached out for him. His frown was worth the hassle. The time it took him to getting around to lift her down, she could have waxed his truck.

She swept her hands down the length of his arms, caressing him as he lifted her down. "I didn't want to hurt myself jumping down," Maggie declared innocently. She held her breath when he pulled her against him and held her.

"No problem," he sighed.

Maggie pressed herself against him and he held his breath. His slow release of air blew across her cheek. The sweetness of his breath and the crisp scent of his aftershave sent her mind in a million different directions. She didn't breathe until her feet finally touched the ground. She held onto his shoulders a moment longer to make sure her legs would hold her.

"Shall we commence having fun?" Paul bowed.

"Show me a good time, sailor." Paul's eyebrow shot up and Maggie blushed.

"Oh, I guarantee it." He took her hand and pulled her toward the crowded street. He bought a pair of masks from a street vendor and led her into the crowd.

Children crowded around them, running hell bent on getting closer to members of the various *krewes* who strolled the blocks. Dirty looking men grabbed at scantily clad women as they passed. People drank beer and ate food out of plastic containers. A small boy in costume, a beignet in each hand, bumped into them as he ran past, his laughter ringing back.

"I can't ever remember having a night like this."

"Well, I'll try to make it memorable."

Reluctantly, she let him lead her into a crowded restaurant. After a short wait, they fought the crowd to get to their table. They enjoyed a muffuletta pizza and hurricanes before venturing back out into the street. Paul put one arm around her and they slipped into the crowd. Bands played on every corner and people danced without inhibitions. The hurricane swept away many of her own misgivings and she found herself enjoying the headiness of the night.

"I'm still hungry." Paul veered to a food vendor cart.

"You're what?" Maggie couldn't even think of food. Stuffed from the dinner they'd just eaten.

Several hands grazed across her bottom and he chalked it up to tight crowds. Just as she reached Paul's side her eye caught something unusual.

"Paul, look over there." She pointed across the street to an alley. A group of men stood between the buildings.

"Greely." Paul slammed his money down on the steel counter and shoved Maggie's sausage into her hand. They stood together watching as the men argued.

Several of the men glanced around nervously. Packston Greely kept his eyes focused off in the distance. Paul recognized two of the men as thugs who'd tried to pressure Holt into paying protection money a while back. They worked the small town areas outside the city. Port Ray seemed a pretty big distance for them. He knew they'd both served time for various crimes, both known gangsters.

"Paul, that short guy is Marcus Ihne. He's one of the bosses out of Shreveport. What do you think he's doing down here?" He didn't seem to hear.

Paul pulled a micro camera out of his pocket and stepped behind the large cart. He clicked off several clear pictures of the group. Once they got their stories written he'd pass the pictures on to the police.

He'd just tucked the camera back into his pocket when Packston turned around and saw him. He pulled Maggie into his arms and kissed her. She struggled against him, but he held her still. Hopefully, Packston didn't recognize them and they could get away. He took several steps to the side and when he was sure they were out of range he let her go.

Her fist jammed into his stomach.

"Oomph!"

"What was that all about?" She poked him again. "We had an agreement and you said you wouldn't force yourself on me again."

Caught up in the moment and distracted by the situation and her violent reaction, Paul wanted to lash out and smack her, but he'd never so much as raised a hand to any female in his whole life. Becky Muir had beat him up once in front of all his friends because he couldn't hit a girl. Maggie was pushing her luck.

Don't flatter yourself, and I've never forced myself on you and you know it."

"Then what was that all about? That's not forcing?"

"Packston was looking at us and I was hoping if he couldn't see our faces he wouldn't recognize us."

Her mouth snapped shut and she lowered her head. "Oh."

"Well, it didn't work." They both turned around to find two of the Greely brothers standing next to them. Maggie felt the point of something up against her side. "Let's go."

"I don't think we're going anywhere with you," Paul argued.

"Miss Howell, would you care to enlighten him on what you want?"

Maggie raised her chin defiantly and in a clear and easily heard voice said, "He has a gun in my side." She smiled when her captor looked around. He waited to see if anyone around them had heard her. No one paid any attention. Packston dug it in a little deeper and Maggie took her cue to go with him. They stopped in front of a small vacant looking trailer at the far end of a construction lot. Packston shoved Maggie up the steps. Paul caught her when she stumbled and Norbert backhanded him.

"How gallant of you, Paul, but then you've always been such a pushover with the women."

Once inside the building, Packston shoved Paul into a chair. Maggie took the opportunity to look around the trailer. There was very little furniture. A desk and several chairs. The kitchen area had dirty dishes stacked on the counter. Flies buzzed around.

"Sit down, Miss Howell. I've got some business to take care of before I take care of you."

Norbert tied Paul's hands behind his back then moved to her. Paul sat up taller and was about to speak. Maggie didn't want to see him get hit again, so she asked the questions she knew was coming. Her mouth was dry and she hoped she could fake some kind of bravery. "What are you moving Packston? Drugs? Weapons?"

"Oh, nothing so dramatic for this trip. We've got some spare car parts lying around and we've decided to sell them for scrap."

"You're transporting stolen car parts across state

lines aren't you?" She saw Paul's warning expression, but ignored him. She wanted to find out as much as she could.

"You know quite a bit for a newcomer to town. Too bad for you. I would have thought you'd find enough in your own neck of the woods to keep you busy. My friend Mr. Ihne was surprised to see you this far South."

"You know Marcus Ihne?" Paul questioned. "Why didn't you tell me before, Maggie?"

Maggie didn't know why he needed to ask, she was covering organized crime, and Ihne sat at the top of the food chain. "I did a story about him last year. He tried to convince Shreveport he was legit. Besides, I told you a little while ago."

"No, you didn't. I would have remembered you telling me you knew a crime boss."

Maggie sighed. "I don't really know him. I did a fifteen minute interview with him."

"How come I never read it?"

"Paul," Maggie exclaimed.

"I'd love to stay and find out how this ends, but I have to go and supervise some work. Norbert will stay with you until I'm ready to take care of you." Without further explanation, he left.

Maggie kept her eye on the window. She nodded to Paul when she saw Francesca creeping toward the trailer. She expected her friend to barge into the trailer and get them all killed, but she didn't. Maggie smiled when she heard the light knocking. Norbert looked out the window.

"Nothin' out there." He heard the knocking again. He opened the door and Maggie watched him fall.

Francesca's smiling face appeared in the doorway. "That's the first useful thing I've done in my entire life."

Paul smiled. "Not quite, but we'll debate that later." Francesca worked the ropes until she got Paul untied. Once he'd freed Maggie, they dragged Norbert inside and hog-tied him.

Together they made their way into the crowd and headed for the truck. Paul insisted Francesca ride with them and he agreed to send someone after her car before Packston could see it. He pulled out his cell and punched in a number.

"Hal, I need to use the dark room." He paused. I know it's your birthday. I don't need you. I just need the key to get in." Another pause. "Fine, Hal. You can come along, but don't you dare tell Eileen it's me. We'll meet you there."

He dialed another number and informed the person on the other end of the line where to find the car and where to find the spare key.

When they got to Hal's studio, Paul filled him in on what was happening while they developed the film. The pictures were clear enough to easily identify all of the men in the group. It wasn't enough to put anyone away, but they had enough material to write a heck of a story. A story that would definitely open some eyes and maybe even open some doors for the police.

"Hey, Paul, there is this new thing called a digital camera. Ever seen one?" Maggie grinned.

"Yeah, I've got one, but nothing beats good old fashioned pictures to prove there wasn't any computer manipulation going on. Too many cases lost on the premise that someone photoshopped in."

Maggie nodded. "Fair enough."

Paul and Hal talked while Maggie made several phone calls. Francesca had long ago fallen asleep in her chair.

"Maggie, how would you feel about sharing the by-line on this story?"

"With who?" She knew with who, but she wasn't going to make it easy for him. His career meant as much to him as hers. It meant a lot to know he was willing to put her name next to his.

"With me, you wench. Hal thinks we should wait a little while to run the story. Let Packston think he's scared us off. That way maybe we can catch him in the middle of something big."

"I'll have to check with Joe, but I don't suppose it'll be a problem."

"Good. We can spend some time together writing it. We can send our information to the police just before we send it to Hal and Joe."

"Shouldn't we do that now?" Maggie asked. She knew, all too well, the consequences of withholding evidence.

"If we do, they'll put the story on hold and we need to get our facts straight before we make any accusations."

"Paul, we were just kidnapped by a mobster!"

"Yeah, I know. I was there. Remember?"

"Don't be cute. We can have Packston in jail within the hour."

Paul stared at her. "And back out within the next."

"Oh." She saw the sense of his logic and felt some of the wind leave her sails. "So what do we do?"

"We'll do the story and they can all handle it as they see fit."

Maggie liked the idea of working closely with him. His kiss on the street had stoked the fire she'd been struggling to keep under control. The only time they seemed to get along was when they were working and that was fine with her. It was as good a place to start as any. They could get to know each other better.

Francesca's car had been delivered to the library and after they had dropped her off and followed her home, Paul headed for his house. He caught Maggie's shiver when they drove past the spot where she'd wrecked her car. He reached out and took her hand in his.

"I'm fine. It's just a little weird. Did I ever tell you thanks?"

"Several hundred times. We're just lucky I decided following you."

"I'm lucky," she said.

"We're lucky."

Maggie let it drop. She was tired and had no desire to embark on one of their sparring matches. All she wanted was a hot bath and a good night's sleep.

"Maggie, don't you think it's time we talk about what happened at the cabin?" Too much had happened in the last week for him to ignore this. He had feelings for her, damn strong feelings, and he had a hunch she did too. Things had changed since she'd stormed into his life and he had no intentions of letting her go without a fight.

"Nothing happened." She looked away. "It was a mistake."

"Which is it Maggie? Nothing happened, or what we both know happened was a mistake?" How could she ignore the chemistry between them? "I know you think you don't like me, but your body says otherwise." *Oops, that didn't come out right.* "What I mean is, there is definitely something between us."

"You're right, there is." She turned and headed for the stairs. "Space." She started up the stairs.

"Wait." Paul rushed after her. He climbed up and stopped one step below her. "Don't walk away. Please. Haven't you done enough of that?"

"Paul, I'm here to do a story, that's it. I don't have room in my life for anything else." She reached up and stroked his cheek. "I just can't do this. Try to understand."

He didn't understand, and he didn't want to. He wanted her, in the worst kind of way. "Tell me you don't want me as much as I want you."

Her cheeks blushed crimson and she looked everywhere, but at him. "That's not the point."

Karen L. Syed

"The hell it isn't. I can't think of a better point. God, Maggie, it's like a brush fire waiting for wind." Paul leaned closer. "Every day I look at you and wonder if God sent you here to torture me."

"I don't mean to. I can't help the way I am." Tears welled in her eyes and she tried to turn away.

"*Oh non, chère*. Not that. It's your eyes that torture me; it's the sound of your voice that drives me wild." He reached out and took her hand. "Don't you know what you do to me?"

"Why are you doing this? Can't you see? I can't love you, I won't." Tears streamed down her cheeks and she pulled away from him.

"Tell me why." He hadn't counted on tears and he didn't think he could handle them.

"I don't belong here. I'm not like you and your family."

Paul listened to Maggie explain about all the things she couldn't give him, but never mentioned the one thing he wanted more than any of them, love. "Can't we take it one day at a time? I don't want to force you to be with me if you don't want to."

"It's not that . . ."

Tired of the fight, Paul stepped away. "I'm sorry I brought it up. I won't bother you again. We can wrap this story up so you can get back to your life." Paul brushed past her and went into his room. This time it was him who slammed the door.

Maggie sat down on the step and buried her face

165

in her hands. How could she stand there and lie to him like that? She'd never wanted anyone like she did him. Every time he came near her she wanted to reach out and touch him.

Then do something about it.

"What?"

Tell him. Show him. You're a big girl; don't you think it's time you took control of your life, instead of hiding from it?

Maggie hated it when the voices inside her head made sense. But maybe it was time she took a risk. She stood and headed upstairs. The top step held two options. She could chicken out and hide in her room, or she could do what she really wanted.

She knocked on Paul's door and waited for him to answer. When he didn't she opened it anyway. He sat on the edge of his bed with his head resting on his hands. He didn't look up when she closed the door behind her. She struggled for the right words to say, to tell him how she truly felt. Show him.

She reached up and stroked his hair. She stopped when he tensed. She started to pull away, but his hand caught hers. He pulled her against him and wrapped his arms around her waist. "I didn't mean to hurt you, Paul."

"I don't know how to make you understand, Maggie."

"I do." Maggie pushed her fingers into his hair and held him tight against her.

"How do I know this is what you want?" He raised

his head and stared into her eyes.

Pain and confusion and desire glistened in his eyes. Maggie sensed the depth of each emotion and drew on them. She lowered her head and softly brushed her lips across his. A soft sigh slipped out and blew across his mouth. A second later, his lips crushed against hers. She opened her lips to him and soared with the desperation in his kiss. Shivers of warning followed each stroke of his tongue. His hands moved down to her legs and one at a time pulled them up around him.

"I want to show you where you belong," he whispered against her mouth.

Maggie turned her face into his neck and took a deep breath. She wanted to belong, more than anything. She pressed her lips against his warm skin and kissed him gently. His head rolled back. She nuzzled his cheek and his day's growth of whisker brushed against her skin.

Paul leaned back onto the bed, never taking his gaze off Maggie. She moved with him, but he pushed her back up. Slowly, he reached up and one by one undid the buttons of her shirt. He pushed the fabric off to expose her thin white bra. He cupped her with his hands and enjoyed the feel of her nipples against his palms, each stroke of his thumb making them harder. He gently squeezed with his thumb and forefinger.

"Ohh." The sound surprised and excited her.

Paul raised himself back up and reached behind her. His fingers fumbled with the hooks, but finally opened the clasps. He slipped one strap, then the other off her shoulders. Impatient for him to continue his touching, Maggie tossed the bra aside. His mouth covered her nipple and she gave in to the feelings. Teasing and tormenting her with his tongue, Paul continued his strike against her senses. He pulled back to stare at her and it occurred to her to be embarrassed, but his hands on her bare flesh distracted her.

Maggie pulled her legs from around him and he stood them up. Nerves tingled to life from the touch of his hands. He pushed the rest of her clothes off, leaving her totally exposed.

"This isn't quite fair."

"What's not fair, *chère*?" The sound of his voice chased shivers along her spine. His hands went thankfully around her waist and she fell against him. "That I have you right where I want you?"

"Well, you seem to be sorely overdressed for the occasion."

"Then why don't you do something about it?"

Maggie smiled up at him. "Is that a challenge, Remington?"

His rich laughter echoed around her, melting her resolve and draining her of any remaining coherent thought. "First we'll get rid of this." She pushed his shirt up over his head and threw it across the room. She rubbed her palms against his chest, smiling when his nipples hardened. She leaned down and flicked her tongue across one. His hands went into her hair and she stopped.

"No, don't stop." He sighed.

Taking the tender flesh gently between her teeth, she nibbled until he arched against her. With each flick of her tongue his breathing grew quicker. "I guess the next thing to go should be these."

With trembling hands, she unbuttoned his pants. The zipper, stretched from his arousal, proved to be more of a challenge. Once she finally had it open, she tugged at the waistband until she could slide the jeans down to the floor, taking his boxers with them. She moved her hand to touch him, but Paul grabbed her shoulders and pulled her back into his embrace. "If you touch me, Maggie, it'll be all over."

His honesty touched her, and she showed him by touching his face. Stubble scratched against her fingers and she enjoyed the masculine feel of him. She pushed against him and he fell back onto the bed. Laying on top of him gave her a sense of power, made her feel more in control of the situation, but she didn't enjoy it as much as she thought. "Make love to me, Paul." She kissed his mouth, then his cheek. She brushed against him as she stretched to reach his neck.

He growled against her throat and rolled over on top of her. He lay still for a moment, struggling to keep control. Nothing would stop him from doing just what she wanted, but he wouldn't do it like a high school kid in the back of his first car.

He took her wrists and pushed them up over her head. She struggled briefly, but gave in when his mouth covered hers. He tasted the remnants of alcohol as he sucked her tongue into his mouth. Without breaking their kiss he moved his hands along her body. Down her arms, along her sides and down to her thighs. He held one hand against her hips and pushed the other one between her legs. He groaned out loud when his hand found her moist and ready.

He slipped a finger inside her and she bucked against him. She lifted one leg up and gave him more access to her most private part. He worked against her, teasing her until she cried out. He pushed her other leg up and moved against her. Unable to wait any longer, he pushed inside her. She arched up to him and pulled him deeper inside her. His eyes threatened to close, but he forced them open. He wanted to watch her. He wanted to see her eyes grow wide with each stroke. He wanted to see the pleasure in her expression with each minute that passed.

His control slipped and he increased the speed of his thrusts. Again and again he pushed inside her, feeling her close around him, taking all he had to give, and giving in return. He pounded against her and she grabbed at his shoulders, her nails digging in.

"Oh, *chère*, I want–" His chest tightened and he pushed against her one last time. He didn't fight the shudders rocking him. Sweat rolled down into his eyes, stinging and momentarily blinding him. Maggie brushed the drops off his forehead and wiped her hand across her chest. "You're wicked."

He pushed against her and they fell back into

rhythm with one another. It didn't take long for Maggie to lock her legs around him. She pulled him down until she could reach his lips and then gave in. Her body shook and quivered. Paul slowed his movement, but didn't stop until she whimpered against his shoulder. He lay on top of her for a few minutes before rolling sideways.

"Don't go." Maggie clung to him desperately. She wasn't ready to let him go.

"I'm not going anywhere." He pulled her to his chest and wrapped his arms around her. "I couldn't even if I wanted to."

"Do you?"

Paul tipped her head up and kissed her full on the mouth. His tongue moved against hers until she couldn't breathe. "I'm exactly where I want to be."

"I'm glad." Maggie lay in his arms struggling to stay awake. She lost the battle and dozed off with her head on his chest.

She tossed and turned, fighting against the pressure in her chest, running from the evil chasing her, and searching for Paul. She sensed him, but couldn't see him, she heard him calling out to her, but couldn't reach him. She pushed up off the bed and looked around the room. Paul's room. She turned her head toward the door and several clumps of damp curls fell down into her face. She pushed them away from her eyes. "Ohh." The muscles in her arms cried out in protest. The events of the night before came rushing back. The disappointment of waking up alone overshadowed the dull ache in all of her limbs. She reached for her clothes, but found a robe instead. She pulled it on and tied the belt around her waist. A black hair band lay on the bedside table and she picked it up. She pulled her hair back before heading for her own room. She heard the shower running and considered joining Paul, but decided if he'd wanted that he would have invited her. She hurried into her room and quietly closed the door.

She curled up under the covers of her bed and hugged her pillow. She decided not to jump to any conclusions until she'd faced Paul. She had been known to overreact.

Paul stood at the foot of the stairs sifting through the mail. He looked up to see Maggie coming down toward him. "Well, why don't you make yourself right at home here?"

Maggie turned and stared at him. "I beg your pardon?"

"Now, you're even getting mail here."

Maggie snatched the envelope from his hands and tore it open. She missed getting mail and wondered if her neighbor had actually bothered picking hers up.

"Anything I should worry about?" Paul stepped closer.

"It's an invitation to a party at Franklin Raynor's mansion. I wonder why Francesca didn't hand deliver it."

"Who knows? These society folk are pretty weird

about this stuff. So, are you going to go?"

"Don't you think I should?"

"On the contrary, I definitely think you should, but not alone."

"Are you fishing for an invitation of your own?"

Paul searched the stack of remaining mail. "It seems as though you're my only hope."

"Why would you even want to go? You don't even like Francesca." Maggie moved across the room and plopped on the sofa.

"That's not true. I just can't help wonder what her ulterior motives are."

"Paul, I thought we were past this. Hasn't she more than proved herself?"

"I suppose. So are you going to invite me or not?"

"If I don't I'll never hear the end of it. But you have to wear a tuxedo."

"I wouldn't have it any other way. I look pretty damn spiffy in a tux.

Maggie had no doubt he was telling the truth. She could hardly wait to find out. "Then it's settled. All I have to do is figure out what I'm gonna wear. I didn't come prepared for a shin dig like this."

"I'm sure you'll scrape up something suitable."

"I'll try not to disappoint you."

Eleven

The invitation sat up against the vanity mirror. Maggie, still unsure whether she should attend or not, held the dress out in front of her. Franklin Raynor was Port Ray's most solid citizen and businessman. Francesca had only touched on his businesses and affiliations.

"Maggie, we have to leave in twenty minutes." Paul's voice echoed up the stairs.

"I'll be ready in ten." She eyed herself in the mirror. Loose curls hung away from the sweep, they weren't supposed to, but she couldn't do a thing with them. She'd kept her makeup light, barely visible, but it worked for her. The big problem was going to be the dress. The shimmering material didn't look like it would be good for much more than a leg warmer. She spun it around and glared at the pearl buttons lining the back, what there was of it.

No sense in putting it off. Maggie let her robe fall to floor and adjusted the garters. Francesca had helped her pick out the opalescent stockings and matching elastic garters. "They're perfect for the dress," she'd said.

Maggie slipped the filmy dress off its padded hanger. The material flowed across her skin like water. The cool sensation sparked a shiver of excitement. Only one other time in her life had she been required to dress up to this degree and one expected that at a congressman's party. She lowered the dress and stepped into it. Wiggling her hips, she pulled it up and slid the straps over her shoulders. Staring at herself in the mirror she couldn't believe it. The person looking back couldn't be her. The reflection looked slim and elegant, attractive, not plain and business like. Maggie had no idea what to do. She stood motionless until she heard Paul's voice. "Your ten minutes are up, Maggie. Get down here."

Rousted from her appraisal she reached behind her to hook the buttons. Her fingers fumbled with the first hook, never catching it. "Damn." She'd have to get Paul's help. Paul, what would he think? He'd probably have some wise comment to make about her choice of outfits. For a brief moment, Maggie wished Francesca were here to smack, but that wasn't fair, she'd wanted to buy this dress, and she'd wanted to look like this. She just didn't know why. Or maybe she wasn't ready to admit it.

She grabbed her small beaded purse off the bed and hurried out the door. When she looked down the stairs, she didn't see Paul. Obviously, he wasn't as curious about her eveningwear as she wanted him to be. She lifted the hem of her dress and moved down the stairs. When she reached the bottom, she saw him standing next to the window seat in all his splendor. She cleared her throat and he spun around to face her.

Paul sat on the window cushion, then he stood back up. He opened his mouth to speak, then sat back down. The track lights over the stairs caught and reflected the opal shades in her–dress. Was it his imagination or was the bare skin of her arms and–chest–sparkling?

"Are you okay?" Maggie stepped toward him.

Paul held his hands out in front of him. The thought of her coming any closer terrified him. He glanced up to the soft curls falling around her face. A face as perfect as anything he'd ever seen. Her cheeks glowed like a pale peach rose in the moonlight. He nearly choked when her tongue darted out and slipped along her upper lip. His heart hammered in his chest like the drums in Congo Square as he gazed down to her midriff and the tanned skin of her sides exposed by perfectly round cut out holes in her dress. A dress that hugged every excruciatingly perfect curve of her body. A body designed for worship. Innocence personified. Devastating beauty and raw sensuality.

"Maggie–you–I've never–"

She turned toward the stairs. "You hate it."

""Maggie, wait." Paul hurried toward her. "You look–exquisite."

"I doubt that."

He noticed the open button lining the flawless curve of her back. "You're not hooked."

"I know," she whispered. "I couldn't reach them."

Paul knew he'd have to help her, but when he looked down at his hands, he didn't think he could. He clasped them together, hoping to still the trembling. He closed his eyes and took a deep breath. Soft lilac wafted around him, making him lightheaded. Everything around him spun, and he reached out for the wall. He opened his eyes to find her staring at him.

"I should change into something–different."

He barely heard her words, whispered out of uncertainness. He couldn't let her change; he wanted to see her in this dress, to be seen with her in this dress. He wanted everyone to know he wasn't a small town boy, who couldn't find class with a road map. Then again, he didn't care what anyone thought about him and his relationship with Maggie.

"No, I'll hook you up." He touched her shoulder lightly and she turned away from him. With each breath she took, her shoulder rose and fell. If she'd only stop breathing, he could concentrate on what he was supposed to be doing. He looked down at the small button and wondered how the hell he was supposed to get them through the small hoops opposite them. He reached down and caught one between his fingers. Fingers shaking so violently he feared ripping the blasted button off. Finally, he got the first one through the elastic ring. Carefully, he worked his way up the row of ten buttons. When he reached the last one, his fingers lingered. His thumb rested against the coolness of her skin. Her sharp intake of breath held him paralyzed. He couldn't pull away. If he lost the touch, she'd disappear. Gently, he rested his open palm against her back and felt her lean into him. His other hand moved up to the bare skin of her side, warm and supple.

"Paul," she sighed.

"Maggie, I'm sorry." He didn't understand why he was sorry. He wanted to touch her, every inch of her and feel her pressed against him. Then she was. One step and her back molded with his. His hand moved up her back and found its way to her neck. He toyed with a stray curl lying at her nape. Her head tilted forward, offering him total access, which he took without hesitation. His lips followed the natural curve of her neck until they reached her ear. Her delicate skin deserved more than his clumsy touch, but he didn't stop. He had to stop.

"We can't do this–"

"I know," he answered.

"No, we can't do this now."

The raspy tone of her voice thrilled him. Warmth flooded him with the knowledge that she wanted him as much as he wanted her. Or at least she wanted him. He brushed his lips along her jaw line and took one more deep breath, taking enough of her to hold him until they could finish what they'd started.

Maggie stepped away from him, but didn't look at him. She needed to regain her composure and she couldn't let him see the tears in her eyes. "I'll get my cape and meet you in the car."

Paul reached over and scooped the thin fabric off the back of the chair. "I've got it." He stepped up to her and wrapped her cape around her shoulders. "Are you okay?"

"I'm fine." She paused. "Thank you." Without another word, she stepped away from him and hurried into the garage. She wiped her eyes and pinched her cheeks before he caught up with her. She waited while he opened the truck door and held her tongue when he grasped her waist and lifted her into the truck. They made the trip across town in silence, sexual tension beating between them with a life of its own. It wasn't until they reached the Raynor mansion that Paul finally spoke.

"Maggie, make sure you don't wander too far tonight. Packston and his goons will be in full force."

Maggie had already thought of this, but Paul's overprotective tone, made her bristle. "I'm quite capable of taking care of myself."

Paul slammed the truck door. "I never said you couldn't. The point is, you don't have to."

A valet parking attendant stepped up and broke the spell of tension between them. Paul handed him the keys and they were lead up a walkway.

The bright white decor of the foyer nearly blinded Maggie. The vividly painted pieces of art hanging on the walls only added to the extreme brilliance. Maggie noticed the spotlights aimed at each piece. She hadn't stepped into a man's home, she'd stepped into a museum someone lived in. Everything impeccably arranged, screamed to be noticed. As the butler escorted them into the main ballroom, Maggie heard their names echo across the room. Within seconds, Francesca stood by her side.

"Maggie, I thought you weren't coming." She took Maggie's hands and stood back from her. "Oh, Maggie, it's even more beautiful on you than I imagined. This dress was made for you."

"Yes, Miss Howell, I believe my fiancé is right. I wish she could wear something so enticing."

Maggie shivered as Paul slipped a possessive arm around her waist. Every muscle in his body tightened. She shrugged away and moved to slip her hand into his, removing his almost painful grip on her.

"I'm sure if she had someone special to dress for she would." Maggie didn't miss the glimmer of tightly contained anger in his dark eyes. She instantly regretted her words when Packston lifted his hand and let it rest on Francesca's neck.

"Oh, but she does." Packston turned his attention away from her and glared at Paul. "Remington, I don't believe I saw your name on the guest list."

Francesca opened her mouth to speak, but a visible squeeze from Packston halted her words.

"Are you adding party crasher to your vast array of–talents?"

"Paul is my escort for the evening. Is there a problem with that?" Maggie wasn't about to let this clown intimidate her. "Besides, I wasn't aware this was your party."

"Oh, but it is, Maggie—can I call you Maggie?"

"Miss Howell will do, if you must call me something."

"This is our engagement party. Franklin will be formally announcing our impending nuptials. She insisted you be present."

"Well, I'm flattered she would think of me for support." The longer they stood here the more annoyed she became. If she didn't get away from him soon, she'd end up doing something they'd all regret.

"If you'll excuse me, I need to find the ladies room."

"I'll go with you, Maggie."

Francesca took her hand and they started to walk away. Maggie went back and leaned toward Paul. "Can I trust you to behave while I'm gone?"

"You can trust me with your life." He brushed his mouth across hers and she hurried away.

Paul watched them walk away, uneasiness swept through him as he lost sight of Maggie.

"So, Remmy, you must be in hog heaven to have a prize like her on your arm." A malicious grin touched Packston's lips as he leered in the direction the women had walked.

"Try not to trouble yourself over my good fortune. I'd say you have other problems to worry about."

Paul watched as the man contemplated his response. "I don't have a care in the world. Things couldn't be better. Francesca may not be as stunning as

Maggie Howell, but she'll serve her purpose."

"You're an evil son of a–"

"Now, now, Remmy, I'd hate to have you ejected from the social event of the season. Although, if you weren't around, I'd personally see to it that Maggie made it home safely–eventually."

Paul leaned into his adversary. "If you go near her or so much as think of it, I'll see you rot in hell."

"Big words, from a small man. You don't have the guts or the means to go against me. None of you ever have. The Greelys have been besting you bayou Remingtons for as long as anyone can remember."

"You wish, Greely. You only think you're better. No one else does."

"None the less, you should be thanking me."

"What for? Making my family suffer for years? Getting in my way at every turn? Do tell, Packston."

His evil laugh echoed out over the crowd. Several guests turned to stare at the two men. Paul watched the sparkle of amusement in his opponents eyes turn to fury. "You don't think that two bit reporter made it this far in her career on her own merit, do you?"

Before Paul could respond, Franklin Raynor stepped into the spotlight. Maggie stepped up next to Paul as Packston hauled Francesca into his embrace. "He's a pig."

"Was there a problem while I was gone?" Maggie looked up at him, waiting for an answer.

"Nothing unusual." He hesitated briefly. "How did you get this assignment, Maggie?"

"What do you mean, how did I get this–"

"Did you ask for it?"

Maggie looked at him, suspicion clear in her expression. "No. I was chosen by the editor and his crew. Why?"

"No reason. I just wondered if this was a clever ploy to meet someone as talented in the field as I am."

Maggie covered her mouth, hiding a smile. "Dream on, Remington."

With the announcement out of the way, the music began and several couples joined Packston and Francesca on the dance floor. Paul swept Maggie into his arms and they melted together in a flurry of spins and dips. Paul held her as close against him as propriety would allow. Her body molded against his in a natural pattern of symmetry. Nothing could have been more perfect than the way they fit together.

They danced, oblivious to everything around them, until well after midnight. Part of the evening they spent on the terrace. The fragrance of the early blooming flowers added to the brilliance of the glowing moon. Glowing lanterns along the garden path illuminated the walkways for couples seeking more privacy. Paul didn't dare take her off alone; afraid he'd never bring her back.

"I think we should head home." Paul couldn't help but wonder if they would pick up where they'd left off.

"I'll just say goodnight to Francesca. You coming?"

Paul was staring off toward a corner of the garden.

"Yeah, I'll catch up. I thought I saw someone I knew." He squeezed her hand and hurried her off.

He slipped down the stone steps and snuck behind a hedge. He couldn't see the faces, but he recognized the gravelly voice of Anthony Greely and the whiny tenor of Michael Pastorelli. He'd caught a brief glimpse of the mafia figurehead earlier, but thought his eyes had been playing a trick on him. It occurred to him that several of the other guests were also known acquaintances to the underworld. He would have chalked it up to the Greelys if not for the presence of Franklin Raynor in the small clandestine meeting.

When the men separated, Paul slipped back inside and gathered Maggie's cape. She stood by the front door, waiting for him. "Sorry, I took so long."

She eyed him curiously before letting him lead her to the main drive. Again he lifted her into the truck. The feel of his hands on her waist brought back other memories. His lips, the scent of his cologne, the feel of his chest against her bare back.

"What do you make of that guest list?"

"I'd say it was a typical social gathering." Paul kept his eyes facing the road.

"Are you going to tell me that Pastorelli is a regular guest at Raynor's parties?"

"Who?"

Maggie laughed. "You are a very poor liar." She reached into her bag and pulled out a small tablet. She read the first page. "Pastorelli, Conti, Marcello, Greely, and ten other mafia boys. Are you going to tell me you didn't notice the bosses mingling like they belonged?"

"Don't you ever do anything but work?"

She watched his grip tighten on the steering wheel. Her mind raced back to their dancing on the patio. "I don't get many chances."

"Is that how you want it?"

"Does it matter?

Twelve

"This is the last thing I need right now."

"Who is it?"

Paul slowed the truck and looked at her. "Whatever you do, don't say anything. No matter what you're asked don't give any answers. I'll do all the talking." He slammed his hand on the steering wheel. "Why didn't anyone tell me?" He made a mental note to sock both of his brothers.

"Why? Paul, you're making me nervous."

The garage door opened and Paul parked the truck. He sat for a long time before climbing out. Her feet had no sooner hit the ground when in the flash of a second she found herself caught up in a whirlwind of chaos.

The house door flew open and a huge hairy beast burst out. All she saw was fur.

"Paul!" Maggie didn't have time to think. She didn't have time to decide what to do next. Her first reaction was to protect Paul. One step put her between the open door and Paul. Whatever it was bounded into her. Then she felt the floor smack her in the back of the head.

She lay perfectly still for several minutes before reaching up to rub her head. Thankfully, she didn't find any blood on her fingers. No thanks to the beast on top of her.

"Dog breath!" Maggie squeezed her eyes closed and held her breath. The hundred plus pounds of fur and slobber bounced enthusiastically on her stomach.

"Bogart, get off! You're gonna drown her."

Maggie suspected he might be right. Warm and disgustingly sticky dog spit rolled down her cheek. She felt the chill of the cool air on her skin as the trail of drool ended at the back of her neck.

"Come here, Bogie. Come to Mama." A shrill whistle bounced off the garage walls and Maggie feared her head would split.

"Mama, you can't do that out here. You'll make us all deaf." Paul's voice sounded distant, as if they were in a tunnel.

Or maybe I'm in the tunnel, Maggie thought. She opened her eyes to find herself still buried under a ton of fluff. The animal hadn't budged so much as an inch since he'd pelted her. His enormous black and white paws were pinned securely on her shoulders. Another stream of doggy drool hung dangerously over her face. Each breath Bogart took threatened to shake the slobber loose. Maggie closed her eyes again.

"Come on, Bogart. Get off." Paul tugged on the sheepdog's collar, but he held fast. "Mama, do something. Maggie is recovering from an accident and we'll be lucky if this fool dog hasn't killed her."

"I'm all right, Paul." Maggie stared up at him. "Just get him off me before that spit falls in my eye and I'm blinded." She saw Paul lean forward and he swept the drool away with his hand.

"Goodness, Mama, can't you ever go anywhere without this dog?"

"I never left you at home because you were a pain in the neck. Why would I leave him?"

Maggie chuckled and Bogart ran his tongue up her cheek. So, Paul had been a handful as a child? Maggie wasn't surprised. Finally, they coaxed Bogart off of her and Paul pulled her up to her feet. She felt her cheeks heat up when he turned her around and brushed the dirt off her backside. "I can do that." She swatted at him.

Maggie stood perfectly still as the strange woman circled her.

"So is this your new *petite amie*?"

Maggie felt a blush heat her cheeks and opened her mouth to answer, but Paul cut her off.

"No, Mama. She's not my girlfriend."

"Well then, *chère*, you need to fix that right away. She is so much prettier than the rest of those skinny little she-devils you have gotten mixed up with."

Paul sighed. "I never once dated a she-devil. And please stop talking about my private life. You're embarrassing Maggie." He looked at her sympathetically, but neither one said anything to her.

Maggie knew she should be annoyed that they were talking about her as if she weren't there, but she couldn't. She smiled at the older woman's Cajun accent. Maggie had known at first glimpse who she was. The picture in the hallway didn't do her justice. She was much prettier in person, but definitely the mother of the Remington's.

"I'm Maggie Howell. Paul and I are working on a story together."

"Is that so? Well, I'm pleased as pretty pennies that he's come down off that high horse of his."

"Mama. Let's not get into this now."

"Nonsense, *chère*. I think pretty little Maggie must be an exceptional woman to make my Pauly forget his silly rules about working with women."

Maggie smiled. She knew firsthand how Paul felt about that, but he had come a long way in a short time. "We came to an understanding, early on. I'm very pleased to meet you Mrs. Remington."

"Oh no, Darlin'. You just call me Paulette." Maggie looked from mother to son. Paul grinned.

"Yes, I was named after my mama. It was also her papa's name."

"Yes, sir'ree. Jean Paul Portierer. He was a fine man and we're both proud to have his name.

"Mama, let's go inside so Maggie can sit down." They all moved toward the door, but Paul stopped. The over-sized sheepdog barreled into the back of his legs and nearly knocked him down. "Oh no you don't, Bogie. You're staying out here for a while. I want to make sure you don't kill anyone."

Maggie led the line into the living room. Once Paulette sat down on the couch, Maggie plopped down into the recliner. Paul went into the kitchen and came back out with a glass of water and a damp towel. Maggie thought he was going to try and wipe her face for her, but he handed her the towel. She wiped the last traces of Bogie off her cheek and draped the cloth across her leg. Paul stood close by. He'd instinctively kicked into his hovering mode.

"Paul. I told you I'm fine."

"Maggie that beast knocked you flat onto a concrete floor. You didn't hit your head or twist your shoulder or anything?"

"Paul, I took on a hell of an accident and won. I hardly think Bogart could do much to hurt me."

Maggie noticed Paulette off to the side. She just sat there watching the exchange. She glanced at Paul who nervously glanced back and forth between the two women.

"Paul, go on out and carry your mama's bags in. I'll keep an eye on Maggie."

Maggie could see him hesitating. In the time she'd spent with him nothing had rattled him quite as effectively as his mother. Not even being kidnapped at gunpoint.

"Go on," she repeated. "They're not going to walk in by themselves."

Maggie found her quaint Cajun accent delightful and she knew right away she was going to like Paulette Remington.

Paul mumbled something about checking his messages first and left the room. Maggie heard the beeps of the answering machine. She sat waiting for her companion to say something. She didn't until Paul had gone out the front door.

"So, tell me about what you and my Paul have got to going on."

Maggie smiled, until she realized what the woman meant by her question. "Oh, no," Maggie stammered. "It's nothing like that. I came in from Shreveport to work on a story with him."

"Oh, posh. I know my boy and you have to have something for him to let you go sleuthing with him. He has definite ideas about women."

Maggie huffed. "Yes, I know, but he didn't let me work with him. My boss sent me and I would have done the story with or without him."

Paulette laughed. "So, that's the way of it. I have a Remmy boy who's met his match. I figured it would be Bonnie Bell who hooked Eric first, but I see you have a good lead on her." She reached out and took Maggie's hand. "You love that scoundrel, don't you?"

Maggie felt her cheeks heat up. "Lord, no. We're just friends. He let me stay here when I had a bad experience at the hotel."

"I see. And there hadn't been none of 'dat *tripotege*?"

"I beg your pardon?" Maggie asked.

"Oh you know, *chère*. That ol' hanky-panky."

There was no way this woman could know about anything between her and Paul and she surely wasn't going to admit to loving him, much less anything else that had happened.

"Don't you fret. I won't tell a soul. A woman has to do what she has to do. I know you must have a plan to get Paul to come to his senses."

Maggie closed her eyes and willed her spinning head to halt. This woman thought she was trying to hook Paul. How ridiculous. The last thing she wanted was to be involved with someone like him. Reality walked in the front door and promptly dropped a suitcase. The other four or five dangled precariously. Maggie's heart went out to him when she saw his face. He was exhausted. The last week seemed to be catching up to him and he looked ready to drop.

"Mama, how long are you staying in town?"

"I don't know. I thought you boys might have missed me."

Paul dropped the rest of the suitcase inside the door and kicked it shut. "Why didn't you go to Holt or Eric's?"

"Do you see how my boy is? No hugs or kiss or nothin'." She turned a pouty lip toward Maggie who smiled at the antics. "Aren't you glad to see your mama?"

"Of course he is. It's just we had a rather trying day with some research. I'm afraid having to take care of me has turned him into a grump." Maggie stood up and maneuvered her way to stand next to Paul. She squeezed his hand and hoped he'd accept it as a sign of support. The look on his face said he was as surprised as she was by the gesture. He squeezed back.

"Nobody made me take care of you. I did it because I wanted to." He looked down at her with the same expression he'd been wearing the last night in the cabin. For a moment, she forgot his mother was in the room. She leaned toward him.

"Well, maybe I should let you two run off to bed." Maggie snapped back away from him. She caught the quick arch of Paulette's brow when Paul stiffened. "I can take care of myself."

"Maggie, go on ahead. I'm going to stay down here and talk to my mother for a while."

"Are you sure? I can stay and talk for a while."

"No, it's fine. I'll see you in the morning."

Maggie smiled and headed up the stairs. It had been a very long day and she had some things she needed to do early in the morning.

"So you two really aren't sleeping together?"

Maggie heard Paul swear in response to his mother's question. She should have stayed down there with him if for no other reason than to save him from all the questions she'd more than likely be the subject of. Then again, she was his mother; he was probably used to it. Maggie closed the door to her room and collapsed onto the bed. She and her mother had never shared a loving relationship. Of course they loved each other, but the hardships and her father took up all the time they should have been sharing. Maggie stared up at the ceiling counting the dots on each square tile until her eyelids grew too heavy to fight. She never even bothered to take off her clothes.

* * *

"Mama, what did you say to Maggie?"

Paulette feigned surprise. Innocence was not her strong suit. Paul knew his family well enough to know that not one of them could mind their own business. It always amazed him that he should be the one who chose reporting as a career. Everyone else was much better at snooping and digging out secrets than he could ever dream of being.

"I didn't say anything." She laid her hand over her chest and batted her thick black lashes at him.

"Don't try that charm stuff with me. I'm immune. Remember?"

"You are gonna break your poor mama's heart. Here I thought you'd be happy to see me and this is the welcome I get." She leaned against the arm of the couch and turned her face away from him.

Charm wouldn't work, but guilt would. "Oh, Mama, you know I love it when you come to visit. I was just surprised to see you so late and all." He sat down next to her and wrapped his arms around her. "How long are you staying?"

"I don't know yet. And it wasn't late when I got here. Where were you?"

"Mama, I'm twenty-six years old. I don't have to check in with you anymore." He rolled his eyes when she stared him down. "I took Maggie to a party."

"And that made her happy?"

Paul let his head roll back against the couch cushion. The stress of the day rushed in and tackled him. He thought of Maggie upstairs in bed. Alone. He pulled a pillow into his lap and hugged it. Partly to fulfill the need to put his arms around something, but more to hide his arousal. "It would have if it weren't for those damn Greelys."

He noticed the wrinkle appear across her forehead. She pulled his hand into hers and kissed it. "Don't be playing with those boys, Paul. You know they're bad news."

"I know, Mama. The trouble is, this isn't playing any more. The stakes have gone up and I don't think they plan on losing."

"Then you get out of the game."

"I can't." Thoughts of Maggie lying in the hospital bed clouded his head. He heard the voice of the Algiers Sheriff telling him the brake lines had been cut and the seat belt release mechanism tampered with.

"What's Maggie got to do with all this? Can you keep that little girl safe?"

Paul turned his head to look at his mama. She knew everything. It had taken him almost losing her to realize how important Maggie was. Yet it took less than an hour for his mama to put all the pieces together. He tossed the pillow aside and pulled his mother into his arms. "I'm sure gonna try, Mama. She means a lot to me."

The phone on the table next to him jangled and he grabbed for it. He picked it up before it could ring again. "Hello."

Holt's voice rambled through the phone line. "I

tried to call you earlier to tell you Mama is in town."

"You don't say?" Paul answered smiling at his mother.

"I couldn't find your cell phone number or I would have used it to track you down. I think she said she was going to go to Eric's."

Paul rolled his eyes. "Well, that would have been good, but things didn't work out that way."

"Uh oh. She's there, huh?"

Paul chuckled at the drop in his brother's voice. "Oh yeah, and just for the record. I think you could have tried a little harder."

"I tried to call. I really did." It struck Paul as funny–darn near ridiculous–how a visit from his mother could strike fear into the hearts of three grown men.

"Well, I'd say you have a valuable lesson to learn from this. I think we can squeeze you in for lunch tomorrow. Let me check."

Paul could feel the tension vibrating through the telephone cord. There were some things you just didn't do to your brothers and he was about to do one of them. He winked at his mother, who sat next to him smiling. She nodded.

"I'm sorry. I have something to do, but mama will pick you up around noon and then you two can spend the whole afternoon together." Paul waited for Holt's response.

"You are a vindictive man, Paul Remington. Give her a kiss for me."

Paul hung the phone up and hugged his mama. She poked him in the ribs. "You know. I think it is pure spiteful that you boys think I don't know about your frantic phone calls when I come to town."

"Mama, you break my heart. He simply called to make sure you'd gotten here safely."

"Posh!" She kissed him and stood up. "Which room is for me? Can I use the guest room?"

"No, Maggie's in there. Use Eric's old room. The bed has fresh sheets." He moved over to pick up the pile of luggage from the front foyer. He struggled up the stairs, barely making it before the handle on one of the bags broke.

Thirteen

Things were no less hectic when Maggie woke to the smell of bacon frying. Bogart had made himself at home on the foot of her bed. She could hear Paul downstairs yelling at someone who wasn't yelling back. And the front door bell was ringing like a church bell on Christmas. Maggie yanked the covers over her head.

"Maggie, *chère*. Breakfast is ready and you can't be sleeping the whole day away." Paulette's voice echoed up the stairs and penetrated through the thick covers.

"Coming," she mumbled back, sure no one had heard her.

"You know, she's a mother and if you're not down there in five minutes she'll come after you with a vengeance."

She peeked out from under the blanket to find Paul standing in her doorway, his arms folded across his chest and a smile as bright as summer on his face.

"I suppose there's no hope for a reprieve?"

"From her? Not a chance." Paul laughed and tossed her robe to her. "She's cooked enough for twenty people and Eric will be here any minute."

"I think it might be a good idea if we worked at your office today. I have a feeling we won't get much accomplished otherwise." Maggie crawled out of bed and wrapped her robe around her. Louisiana mornings were barely chilly, but she needed the warmth. When she turned back around Paul was still standing in the doorway. His gaze had turned from playful to searing and she felt naked beneath his scrutiny. She pushed a few stray hairs away from her face and wiped away any possibilities of sleep from her eyes.

"I'm amazed."

"At what?" Maggie asked genuinely curious.

He stood straight and tucked his hands in his pockets. "You are breathtaking even straight out of bed."

Maggie blushed and lowered her eyes. Before she could deny the compliment or say anything else he turned and walked away. She ran to the mirror over the dresser and stared at her reflection. Sleepy green eyes and hair that resembled a rat's nest. He needed a few more hours sleep and an eyeglass prescription. She grabbed some clothes and scurried into the bathroom. Paulette stood outside the door when she emerged.

"I wasn't sure if you heard me call or not." She took Maggie's hand and led her down the stairs. "You had a package delivered a few minutes ago."

"A package?" Paul heard his mother's words and saw Maggie's face pale.

"What did you do with it, Mama?" Paul was out of

his chair and next to Maggie in a flash. A sharp rap on the front door startled them all.

"Paul, what's the matter? Did I take something I should have refused?"

Paul patted his mother's hand reassuringly and shook his head. Maggie stared up at him. Her face looked determined, but her eyes flashed with fear. Very few people knew she was staying at his house and anyone who mattered had no reason to send anything. "Where is it?"

Paulette scurried to the foyer and retrieved the package. She stopped long enough to open the front door.

"Mama," Paul shouted. "From now on you make sure you look to see who it is before you open the door to anyone." She stared at him wide-eyed and open-mouthed.

"Don't you talk to me like that."

"Mama, I mean it. There are things you don't know and if you can't do as I say then you need to go and stay with Eric." Paul snatched the packet away and stormed into the den. He ignored Maggie when she stepped into the room. The package was flat and he felt relatively certain it didn't hold anything physically dangerous.

"Do you mind if I open my own mail?" Maggie asked.

"Yes, I do. Once I'm sure it's okay, you can have it."

"Paul this is ridiculous. It's probably from Joe. I do

get mail on occasion."

"Is that why you nearly passed out when Mama said you had a delivery? I know what you were thinking and I'm making sure we don't have any more surprise presents for you." He carefully opened the envelope and pulled out the stack of papers. Shuffling through them he decided they were safe. He handed the stack to Maggie who had resumed the role of the extremely irritated Ms. Independence. She opened the folded slip of paper that lie on top and read it.

"Oh my God."

Paul instantly regretted not reading it. He stood up to take it away from her, but she took the papers and fled. Moments later, he heard her bedroom door slam shut.

He walked past his brother Eric who was being force fed by his mama and headed up the stairs. He ignored the questioning gazes that followed him.

"Maggie, open the door." He pounded again. "Maggie, if you don't let me in, I'm going to kick the door down."

"Go away." He heard the crack in her voice and knew she was crying. As close as he could figure she'd got news that something horrible had happened. How the hell did she expect him to comfort her if he couldn't get in? Then he realized that's what she was avoiding.

He'd seen her vulnerable too many times and she didn't want it to happen again. She was hiding from him. He leaned his head against the door. He closed his eyes when he heard the sobs from inside the room. He couldn't just leave her there.

"Maggie, at least tell me what's wrong." He banged his fist against the door. "Whatever it is, let me help you with it."

"You can't, it's done. Now go away."

"I'm counting three and then the door goes down. One–two–"

He heard the lock click, but the door remained closed. She'd taken away his reason to smash in, but she hadn't invited him in. He couldn't invade her privacy and force her to trust him. It went against everything he believed in. He wanted–no, needed–more than anything to be there for her, but she had to want it, too.

"Fine, Maggie. You know I want to help, but you have to trust me. I can't make you let me in, but I'm not going anywhere. I can help you if you let me." He turned away and walked to his own room.

Maggie heard his door close. Softly. Not a slam like she was so used to doing. She'd given him the chance to come in and take control and he hadn't. He'd given her the space she needed. She'd learned enough about Paul to know he was a protector. He would fiercely defend anyone he loved. Love? Was it possible he could love her? She stared at the papers strewn out in front of her. Bogart lay with his head in her lap. The dog had already stolen a chunk of her heart and he was there for her. Protecting her like Paul wanted to. Why could she let Bogart in, but not Paul?

She reread the few lines scrawled across the sheet of paper. I know who killed your father. Meet me at warehouse #4 at midnight and I'll tell you what you need to know.

She couldn't let Paul know about this. She couldn't risk putting him in danger. She had to protect him. No matter what the cost. She'd go to the warehouse alone and then, once she got the information, she'd share it with Paul. Until then, she just had to stay away from him. She didn't think she could withstand the hypnotic effect his eyes had on her if he took a mind to argue it out of her.

Maggie spent the better part of twelve hours hiding out. More times than she could count she heard Paul outside her door. He didn't knock and he didn't come in. She scanned the papers well over a hundred times. She wracked her brain trying to remember any part of her past that would prove or disprove their validity. The only thing that didn't add up was the money.

Her mother always had plenty of money. They lived in a nice home and she always had everything they needed. She didn't live like the other kids whose fathers were truckers. Could it be possible? Had her father worked as a runner for Anthony Greely? The only way she would know is if she asked him herself. She knew the papers weren't from him. After hours of deliberation, she decided not to go and meet whoever was out to destroy her. She'd go straight to the man himself.

Just short of midnight she heard the phone ring. Paul closed the den door and she sneaked past him. She pulled her coat up around her chin. The moon shone full and bright and she shivered under its eerie glow. She swore to herself that once she knew the truth she would share everything with Paul. Maybe once her life was in order she could let him in. Until she knew for sure, she had nothing but excess baggage to offer him. It didn't matter that she loved him with every breath she took. It didn't matter that she'd never felt that way about anyone. She hadn't even loved her parents as much as she loved Paul. When she got back from her meeting with Tony Greely she'd tell him so.

Paul heard the door click, but didn't stop listening to the voice in the phone. His hand held the phone so tight his fingers ached. He remained silent.

"She knew all along that her father worked for Greely. She used you to get to them. It's all about revenge."

Paul finally found his voice. "Who are you and why are you telling me this?" He swallowed past the lump in his throat and dreaded what he knew he had to do.

"She's gone to meet Ihne. She made a deal with him. If she helps him destroy Greely he'll tell her the truth about her father's murder. They're meeting at the warehouse at midnight." The line went dead.

A hideous buzzing roused him from his stupor and he threw the phone across the room. Somebody was lying to him and before the sun came, up he'd know who. Thankfully, his mother had stayed at Holt's for the night so he didn't have to worry about her. He raced up the stairs to Maggie's room. Without knocking, he stormed in. He knew she wasn't there. He'd heard her leave.

He spotted the stack of papers on the desk and grabbed them up. There were police reports about the accident her parents had died in. There was a coroner's report saying there were drugs in his blood. Page after page he read the horrible truth about the Greely's participation in Maggie's parent's deaths. His heart went out to her. And at the same time he cursed her. Why couldn't she trust him? Why had she lied to him and made him out to be the fool? If she had been up front with him he could have helped her find the truth without selling herself out to Ihne.

Paul knew what it meant to be one of the Greely's victims. His entire family knew. He'd been sixteen before he'd ever learned the truth. Anthony Greely stopped at nothing to have what he wanted, including another man's wife. Even the penalty for rape did nothing to scare him. Even now he wondered if Greely's rape of his mother had caused his father to leave them. No one would ever know. He thought of his mother's suffering and hated his father for not trusting her. Why couldn't Maggie trust him? Why couldn't anyone trust?

He lowered his head and fought against the anger welling inside him. He noticed the scrap of paper lying on the bed and snatched it up. The caller had been right. She'd gone to meet Ihne. "God, Maggie. How could you do this?" He sat down and fought for air. Knowing it had all been part of a bigger plan, his heart ached. He'd have done anything for her. "Anything."

Tires squealed as his truck sped down the road. Paul had no control. He was close to losing everything that mattered to him and he wasn't ready to let it happen. He'd have to stop her, prove to her he could help and tell her he loved her. That would fix everything. It had to. The truck screamed around a corner and he saw the warehouse looming in front of him. He slammed on his brakes. His front tire hit a puddle of oil and the truck slid sideways.

"Get a hold of yourself, Remington. You won't do her any good if you're dead." His voice sounded hollow and frantic. He had to calm down or he'd end up getting them both killed. He held his breath and counted to ten. Then he did it again. He scanned the area for Maggie's car. When he didn't find it, he figured she must have hidden so they wouldn't see her coming. The element of surprise. "That's good, Maggie." He climbed out of the truck and headed for the abandoned building.

When he got close enough he saw a faint light flickering in an upstairs window. Carefully, he scaled the fire escape and forced himself through an open window. Once he got his feet planted firmly on the ground he looked around. The room he'd entered was completely empty. Not even a broken piece of furniture. He moved quietly into the hallway. After checking several of the vacant offices he heard a faint shuffling.

It took his eyes a moment to focus when he opened the door.

He stiffened when the cold steel pressed up against his cheek.

"Well, well, well. What have we got here?"

Fourteen

"What a surprise, Miss Howell. However, I have to admit I thought you would have the decency to call at a more respectable hour."

Maggie stood in the middle of Anthony Greely's office. She hadn't known what to expect, but he wasn't it at all. Sitting less than five feet away from her was a crime boss. A man who could decide the fate of another human being. The man who had allegedly had her father killed. Only he wasn't strong, or larger than life. He sat hunched over in a wheel chair barely able to hold his own head up.

His low gurgling cough made her want to wretch. He held his chest as the cough escalated into a full-blown fit. A giant of a man entered the room and gave him an injection. Within minutes, his hacking had subsided and he once again stared at her.

Even though he was obviously very ill and incapable of hurting her physically, she saw something in the steel of his eyes. The man before her held an enormous amount of power and she knew beyond a shadow of a doubt he could crush her like a bug. "I want to know the truth."

"And what truth would that be, my dear?"

Maggie moved closer, but stayed out of reach. "Did my father work for you? His name was Matthew Howell." Maggie barely choked the words out.

"I know who he was. I also know who you are. I make it point to know everything about my employees."

"So, he did work for you." There was no relief in the truth. Only more questions. "Did you have him killed?"

"You are very direct. Unlike your father. Had he told me of his financial difficulties I would have willingly helped him."

"We didn't need your money. My father gave us everything we needed. He worked hard." Her defense of her father sounded shallow and she hoped he didn't see the truth. Oh, he'd provided for them, but their life had lacked so much. All she'd wanted, or needed for that matter, was the love. The money didn't matter.

"Your father was a fool. I paid him twice what he was worth and then he got greedy."

"My father was anything but greedy," Maggie argued.

"Your father stole from me." His words were cold and unfeeling. "He stole several hundred thousand dollars from me."

Maggie felt the tears welling up and she collapsed onto the sofa behind her. "You're lying. You're an evil man and I don't believe any of this."

"Of course you do. Where do you think he got the

money for the fancy truck he bought? Where do you think he got the money for all the trips he took?"

"He didn't take trips. He worked too many hours." That's why he was never home. He was working."

"I was told you were a clever girl. It seems my sources were sorely mistaken."

Her chin went up and she wiped the tears away. "Did you kill my father?"

He looked at her for what had to have been hours before he spoke. "I simply made a comment to an associate that he had betrayed me and stolen from me." He reached for a glass of water and when he fell short Maggie stood and handed it to him.

"You did."

"The merchandise your father sold was not mine to sell. I merely did what I thought best."

"You're a murderer. You took away everything that mattered to me. You killed both my parents and left me an orphan."

He lowered his head. After another brief coughing spell he looked up at her. The same coldness she'd seen before lingered beneath something else. The flash of sadness passed and he pulled himself up taller. "I did what I thought needed to be done. I am deeply sorry for your loss. It was never intended you should lose both of your parents."

Maggie held herself in check. She couldn't lose control now. She had to get him to say he'd killed them or hired someone to do it for him. The tape recorder felt hard against her leg as she shifted. She tucked her hand in her pocket and felt the slight vibration.

"I'm very tired, Miss Howell and I have told you all you need to know." He rang a bell that hung on his chair and the giant man came back into the room. "Elias will come back and see you out once I am situated. Help yourself to a drink. You look like you could use it." He disappeared with his nurse.

Maggie collapsed onto the sofa. She had come wretchedly close to crying moments early, but the urge was gone. Anger replaced it. An anger she knew had always been there, but had fought to ignore. She was angry at her father. Deep in her heart, even as a child, she knew something wasn't right. Only now did she realize for the first time it wasn't her fault.

Her father had worked for a criminal and then he'd stolen from him. It was her father's fault she was alone. Not hers. All the years of mourning his death had been in vain. He'd made his own bed then forced her to lay in it. Even after his death.

Years of anguish and self-pity folded in. Anger lashed out and fear swept through her. She stared dumbly at the walls of the office. It occurred to her where she was and she stood up to run.

"Maggie, what are you doing here? I thought you were–"

"You thought I was what?" Maggie asked, her surprise subsiding.

"Not what. Where. I heard Packston on the phone and he said you were meeting Marcus Ihne at a warehouse."

"How would he know that?"

"Maggie, that's not important. He told Paul."

The fear in Francesca's eyes said all she needed to know. They'd been set up. They had both been led to the warehouse. She knew exactly why. Only she hadn't gone. She hadn't trusted Paul enough to tell him the truth and now he was on his way into the middle of an ambush. She had let him down and now his life was in danger.

"Oh my God, Francesca. We've got to go after him and stop him before they do something horrible to him."

"Packston left a little while ago and he ordered me to be here when he got back. I tried to call you, but no one answered."

Maggie grabbed her hand and they ran out of the house together. Since Francesca knew where the warehouse was, she drove. It took only a few minutes to get there. As soon as they pulled around the corner Maggie saw Paul's truck.

"Please don't let me be too late," Maggie pleaded. She scurried out of the car before it even stopped. Francesca joined her and Maggie ran hell bent toward the back of the building, pulling Francesca along behind her. When she heard footsteps she stopped and pulled Francesca into the shadows of the alley. Her heart fell into her chest when she heard their conversation.

"Get out of here as fast as you can. Don't say anything to anyone about this. Not even my brothers."

Maggie recognized Packston's voice and she felt Francesca tremble against her.

"In five minutes this building is going to be kindling. I'll be rid of part of the problem and I'll collect the insurance money on top of it."

"As far as anyone will know it will be an electrical fire sparked by an unforeseen accident."

Maggie listened carefully, trying to recognize the unfamiliar voice.

"Best of all, I'll be rid of Paul Remington." The two men separated and Maggie waited for the sound of their cars to disappear.

She and Francesca ran into the building as fast as their feet would carry them. Desperate to find Paul, Maggie ran from room to room. She searched behind every door. Finally, she burst into a room and saw him. He sat blindfolded and tied to a chair, his head hanging to one side. At first she thought he was dead then his head bobbed. She noticed the blindfold and his shirt had blood on them.

"Did you come back to finish me off?" His throat sounded dry and his voice raspy.

Maggie ran up behind him and struggled to untie his hands. As his hands fell free he turned and faced her. He reached out to hold her, but she scurried away.

"Maggie."

"No, Paul, we have to get out. We have less than two minutes before this whole building goes up in flames."

Shaking off the stiffness in his arms and legs he

looked at her and they ran off together. The heat wrapped around her and threatened to choke her as Maggie searched frantically for Francesca. Her feet slipped on the slick metal surface of the stairs as she ran down them. She collided with her friend as she reached the bottom of the last flight of stairs. Suddenly, the floor began to rumble beneath their feet. A series of explosions urged them forward.

Paul grabbed both women as they rushed toward exit. The intensity of the pursuing heat burned against her back as Paul pushed her in front of him. No sooner had they emerged, than another explosion ripped through the basement of the building. The pressure blew them forward and Paul tucked himself around Maggie as they rolled along the concrete.

Maggie opened her eyes and tried to find Francesca who had rolled and landed several yards away from them. "Francesca, where are you?" She felt Paul's hand on her arm as she crawled to get away. Her heart raced and horrible images flashed in her mind.

"I'm here Maggie. I'm okay."

Another explosion blasted into the night and Maggie leaned against Paul's comforting shoulder. He pulled her close and she clung to him as they watched the flames blaze up against the backdrop of the midnight sky. Silently, they watched the building cave in on itself.

"We could have been killed in there."

"But we weren't." Paul pulled away and looked down at her. "How did you know about the explosion?"

The lines across his forehead confirmed the tension she heard in his voice. She wondered if it was anger or weariness. The soot and grime smeared on his face gave him a deranged look. A look that frightened her. "I heard Packston outside before I came in."

"Why weren't you here when I got here? Greely was surprised you didn't show up."

"I had something more important to do." Still hesitant to tell him she'd gone to see Tony Greely, she held off saying what.

"I guess you won't tell me about that either, huh?"

Maggie sensed his hurt and knew she had to make it right.

She opened her mouth to speak, but the wail of sirens stopped her. Seconds later, a trail of fire engines and police cars filed into the parking lot. Within seconds they were surrounded by officers asking them a torrent of questions.

Once the reports had been given and everyone had been checked by the paramedics they headed home. Francesca drove her car and Paul and Maggie followed in his truck. When they left her at the front security gate, none of them noticed Packston lurking in the shadows.

"Well, wasn't it nice of them to see you home?" His voice sounded soft, but the menace was clear. "I looked for you at home, but you'd already gone."

"What are you doing here?" She backed away

from him, but he kept moving forward.

"I told you to wait for me. I realize times have changed, but I still expect obedience from my wife." He grabbed her arm.

She tried to squirm away from him, but he held tight. "I'm not your wife and never will be. I know what you tried to do to Paul and Maggie and I wouldn't marry you if you were the last man on earth."

His eyes glowed with a feral gleam. He pulled her roughly against him and in his state he seemed oblivious to the fact that he was drooling on her. She yanked away and turned to run. But he grabbed her by the tail of her shirt and she tumbled to the ground. "Packston, leave me alone or I'll have you arrested."

Hideous laughter rang out, chilling her to the bone. He lunged down on top of her and pinned her to the ground. Unable to breathe or move, she feared he would rape her where she lay. But before he could do anything his body flew off her. She heard Packston groan as his body thudded against the hard earth.

"Miss Raynor, I saw a prowler on the monitor and came out to investigate."

Francesca crawled to the security guards feet and he helped her to stand. Packston lay motionless on the ground. For the second time in hours, she was surrounded by police. She struggled through her explanation of Packston's connections to the latest string of troubles. Packston flung a string of curses at her as the police read him his rights and handcuffed him. A large officer pulled him toward the cruiser, but she stopped them.

"Before you go anywhere, I want you to know something." The evil look in his eye etched itself in her mind. "I will however testify against you, since I overheard several of your phone conversations."

He lunged for her, but the officers and the handcuffs stopped him. "This is not over, Francesca. You owe me and I'll have what is rightfully mine. Mark my words."

"It is over. I'll see you rot in jail if it's the last thing I do." With a sense of relief, Francesca walked the short distance to her front door. The porch light flashed on and she wondered if maybe it might be the light at the end of the tunnel. Maybe she could have a life.

Across town Maggie and Paul stood in his living room staring each other down. "Maggie, I want an answer."

Maggie stood her ground and sighed. With her arms folded across her chest, she patiently waited for him to calm down. He'd yelled at her the entire way home and she hadn't had a chance to say anything.

"Damn it, Maggie. I'm talking to you. I expect you to say something. You can't just stand there looking at me like that and think I'll forget about all this mess. You nearly got me and yourself killed and you are going to tell me–"

"I love you." Her words were soft and simply stated.

"I don't want any excuses-"

"I said, I love you."

"I have gone out of my way to help you and I think you at least owe me-"

"Shut up, motor mouth." That stopped him.

"I beg your pardon. What did you say?"

"I said shut up-"

"Before that." He stood in front of her, his eyes wide and his mouth even wider.

"Oh that," she drawled.

"Yes that!" He moved toward her. "Say it again."

"I love you." Suddenly he crushed her in a flurry of movement. His arms gathered her up and his mouth pressed against hers. She pushed against his chest and he finally released her from the soul-searing kiss.

"I need to tell you some things and I need you to listen to me without saying anything."

He pulled her against him and kissed her soundly on the mouth. "Fine, but be quick about it."

"I didn't tell you about the meeting because I didn't want you to feel like you had to protect me. I wanted to handle it on my own.

"Why?" he asked.

"Since I met you, I seem to have forgotten that I can."

He tried to pull her into his arms, but she resisted.

"I also didn't want to put you in danger."

His eyebrow shot up and he flashed her a roguish grin. "So you were protecting me?"

"Yes," she answered shyly.

"It's all right for you to protect me, but I can't do

the same? I hardly think that's fair."

"I know, and I see that now. I've just had so many years of one thing, I wasn't prepared for all the feelings I had for you. They scared me."

"And you don't like being scared?"

She nodded her head. "Not at all."

"Don't you know we could have saved ourselves a lot of trouble if you'd just trusted me?"

"You're right."

"Don't argue–what did you say?"

"I said, you're right. I should have come to you. But just so there is no misunderstanding, I do trust you."

"Well, that's good. I'd hate for the woman I love to not trust me."

"You love me?"

"Good Lord, Maggie. How could I not? You came into my life like a bolt of lightning and sparks have been flying ever since. Can't you feel them?"

Maggie felt her cheeks blush. "I thought it was my overactive imagination."

He pulled her into his arms again and his lips brushed against hers as he spoke. "Does this feel like your imagination?"

"No," she murmured as she leaned into his kiss.

By the end of the night Maggie had told him everything she'd learned. As they sat together on the sofa it occurred to Maggie that for the first time in her life she was genuinely happy. She had everything she could ever dream of. Almost everything, she thought.

She tugged out of his embrace and lowered herself to the floor in front of him. She looked into his eyes and knew what it meant to be hopelessly in love.

"Paul. You have given me something I never dreamed possible. I never thought I could ever love like this. I didn't think it was in me."

"It's always been there. You just had to believe in yourself."

"I do now. That's why I need to be sure I always have faith in myself and my decisions. You taught me how to give in and now I want to give back."

"You have. It had to be hard for you to say you loved me the way you did."

"It's the easiest thing I've ever done. And it gives me the strength to do this." She lifted his hand and kissed it.

"Do what?"

"Paul Remington, will you marry me?"

His head rolled back and laughter shook his chest. She sat on her knees in front of him, the air slowly slipping out of her self-esteem.

"Good Lord, woman, I do love you."

"Then why are you laughing?"

"You took an age old tradition and twisted it around to suit you. I've hooked myself one hell of a woman."

"So then, answer my question."

He pulled her up into his lap and kissed her soundly. "Yes, Ms. Independence I'll marry you. By the light of the moon, I will."

Fifteen

"You may kiss the bride."

Standing in front of her was the most wonderful man in the world; kind, gentle, understanding and tolerant. Tolerant of all her ideas, as well as her mistakes. He'd become everything to her, friend, lover, and husband. Maggie tried to put all the pieces together. How had she come to be standing in front of a group of people waiting for a kiss, from her husband?

"I love you."

Paul whispered the words so softly she felt them more than she heard them. They wrapped around her, encompassing her with the strength of existence. Then he kissed her.

Softly at first, gentle as if afraid she might shatter. Then she heard the cheers from the congregation. The applause tripped his male ego and he lowered her in a dramatic dancer's dip, igniting the usual passion of their kisses.

"I now introduce to you, Mr. and Mrs. Paul Remington." The minister smiled as he urged them up the aisle.

An hour later, they stood on the porch of their

rented cottage and watched the limo with the tinted windows whisper down the dirt path. Paul pulled Maggie into his arms and showered her with kisses until she giggled and pulled away.

"I have something for you."

"What do you mean; you have another present for me?" Maggie stared at her new husband. His handsome features enhanced by the moon sparkling in his eyes under its glow. Love swelled in her heart.

"I had to do some hard thinking and it cost me my soul, but I found the perfect gift for you."

"So where is it?" Maggie pulled Paul's hands out. Finding them empty she frowned. "Come on. Show me." She bounced around him, still excited from their earlier nuptials.

"We have to do this my way. Come sit down with me, *chère*." He took her by the hand and led her to the swinging seat on the far end of the porch.

He sat long ways with one leg up on the seat, pulling her down in front of him. Maggie eased into the comfortable curve of his arm and let the warmth of his body ease the anxiousness she felt. If anyone had told her six months earlier she'd be married and happy about it, she'd have laughed in their faces. Reluctant professional desire had led her to Port Ray and she couldn't imagine being anywhere else. Paul tightened his arm around her and her heart raced.

"So, tell me what my present is. I can't stand surprises. You know that."

"I know you'll have to learn some patience if you

want to be with me." She swatted Paul's hand. His chest rumbled with laughter.

"Very funny. You're stuck with me, whether I'm patient or not."

Maggie relaxed, watching the clouds scoot across the sky. She couldn't ever remember noticing the sky. She closed her eyes, trying to imagine how she'd seen the moon as a child. Her mind formed replicas of paintings and pictures, but no real images. *How can I not know what the moon looks like? I'm twenty-six years old.*

"How do you like it?" His voice whispered soft and very close to her ear. A shiver ran the length of her spine, an exquisite feeling. Love. The feeling encompassing her was love. Pure, sweet, and wonderful love.

"How do I like what?"

"How do you like being married? I mean is it horrible? Are you sorry you got involved?"

She turned around and faced him. His mouth was smiling, but doubt shadowed the usual twinkle in his eyes.

"Oh, Paul. I've never been happier in my life."

"Really?"

Her heart exploded, sending shards of brilliant emotion to her brain. She reached out with trembling hands to caress his cheek. "Ever since my parents died, I've felt lost, like I don't belong anywhere. I finally found some peace when I started working for Joe. He's all the family I have now."

"Had."

"What?"

"Had. He's all the family you had. Now you have me and my family."

More love. She wondered, could a person die from too much love? God, what a way to go. "Yes. I do. That's what I'm trying to say. From the moment I saw you, I couldn't get you out of my mind. Now I'm married to you and I don't think I will ever be able to tell you or show you how much I love you."

"Family can be a real pain. With three brothers I can't even imagine being lonely or feeling out of place. Even though we don't get to see Jason, he's still our brother and that means something to us."

"Do you think he got your message?"

"I sent it to the post office box and the rest is up to him. Oh, I think it's about time to give you your gift."

Maggie perked up and she felt her cheeks heat up. She felt like a schoolgirl waiting to see which boy would give her the first valentine. Paul pulled her back into his arms. An overwhelming sense of contentment told she belonged there. She knew she would forever belong in his arms.

"Close your eyes." Maggie tried to turn round, but he stopped her. "Just close them. I'm going to have to work on getting you to follow instructions a little bit better."

"Stop picking on me and give me my surprise." The anticipation crawled over her flesh and she peeked one eye open just in time to see the moon start to move out from behind a cloud.

"Okay, open them and look up at the sky." She looked up. "I'd like you to meet someone."

Maggie leaned her head over and looked at Paul. "What are you talking about?"

"I want to introduce you to the man in the moon."

"Paul, you're not making any sense. I've seen the moon and there's no–." Maggie stopped. She turned her head back up toward the sky and stared at the moon.

Gray clouds mingled around the glowing sphere, softening the brightness and adding a haze that made her think of angels. Paul touched her cheek. She leaned into his palm and sighed.

"I wanted to give you something so wonderful you would never get a better present."

"But I don't understand."

"You once told me you didn't have time to stare off into space. You said the moon would always be there so why take time to stare at it. Have you ever seen the man in the moon?"

"I guess not," Maggie answered, staring up at the sky. She studied each blemish. Watching the cloud surface clear away to leave the moon totally unconcealed. At first she couldn't be certain, then she realized with a surprise that there was an eye. She refocused and there was another. Then she saw the tilted point of a nose and a smile. "He's smiling at us."

Her voice echoed with awe and utter amazement. Paul felt her entire body relax against him, and he knew he had succeeded in his task.

"It's incredible. How come I never knew about this?"

"Maybe no one ever loved you enough to introduce you." Maggie turned and smiled at him. She still didn't understand his gift. "Maggie. I'm giving you the man in the moon."

"You can't do that."

"I most certainly can. I'm giving you the moon as a token of what you deserve. From this day forward you will be my wife. You will, until the day time doesn't exist, have two things that are yours and yours alone."

"What?" Maggie asked softly.

"You'll have me as your friend, and your lover. Your husband. And you will have the man in the moon. No matter where you are one of us will always be looking after you. You will always belong with me and he as your friend will shine down on us until everything ceases to exist."

"You are the most wonderful man in the world. I've never in my life had anything so wonderful happen to me."

"Get used to it. And one more thing. Don't ever forget that you are loved and you belong with me. I had to swear to all the angels that I would love you forever or they wouldn't let me give you the moon."

"I hope it's a promise you intend to keep."

"Always."

Karen L. Syed is the president and COO of Echelon Press, LLC. Every day is a new success story for her as she continues to grow herself and her business. She has seen seven of her own novels published (writing as Alexis Hart), along with numerous articles and short stories.

She is committed to helping and encouraging everyone she comes in contact with to seek a healthier and more positive quality of life by reaching for their dreams. She does this with her companies, Echelon Press and Sassy Gal Enterprises.

Her newest fascination has taken root in the Steampunk industry. This tremendously interesting genre based in the Victorian era is helping to feed a minor obsession with the time period. She is currently embarking on her own Steampunk series called *Petticoat Junction*. With more than a quarter of a century experience in the book industry, she hopes this one will propel her into the bestseller category. Time will tell.

Karen recently moved to Orlando, FL with her nearly perfect husband, so they could be closer to Tinker Bell, oh, and Mickey Mouse. She has begun seriously collecting Disney Tinker Bell Trading Pins. She has her priorities in order.

You can learn more about Karen Syed at http://klsyed.com.